Lifeguard Jill talking to Anne in water

Girl Blog From Tucson

Anne Wilensky

And on the 8th day of Chanukah Anne published this book

Published by Haiku Helen Press
Drawing on cover front & back by Billy Stampone
Cover designed by Helen Kritzler aka Haiku Helen

Drawings and cartoons in book by Billy Stampone

To order this book
Go to www.createspace.com/3405361
Or order on-line or ask your local bookstore

ISBN
978-0-9840976-1-6
0-9840976-1-9
Library of Congress Control Number: 2009942343
Printed in the United States of America

Thank you

I want to thank everyone in New York and everyone in Tucson

Ya'll have been very good to me

I have been helped in infinite ways by all of you, and this includes everyone I have been on internet forums with

I am very fortunate

I love you

Anne

Thank you Bill for making it all happen for me

Thank you Eddie for being a writer's angel

Thank you very much to everyone who read my first book "Ruthie Has a New Love" and who liked it. You encourage me. I dedicate this book to you, I hope you like this one also.

for all

I send you our beautiful Arizona sunshine, our flawless blue skies. Let every day come up roses for you.

All my love, Anne

Chapters

Alice

Afternoon at Alice's House

Adventure at Access TV

Old Forge

How it all started

Nancy Cantor

My Trip to Patagonia Lake

Gene

Under the desk with Ruthie

My Yesterday

Steve's Great Writers Meeting Last Night

Room service at Dracula's castle

I decide to publish a book

George and his secretary

I go to Republican BBQ Party

Swim on cold rainy Easter Saturday

Jim wins 3 dollars at lottery

Life Turns Upside Down

I am going to the authors lunch at the Plaza Hotel

6 AM

Today is 3rd Sunday of the month buffet lunch for 20 dollars of the Southwest Authors Society and Sophia and I are going to go. She picks me up at 11 am because it is 11:30 to 2:30. I don't want to spend 20 dollars for lunch but that is the price of admission. I'm sure Sophia doesn't want to spend it either, both of us are budgeting these days, but we are also both serious about wanting to find a way to get our work out into the world.

And Steve who runs our writers group at Barnes & Noble says going to the Southwestern Authors Buffet Lunch at Plaza Hotel on the 3rd Sunday of every month is the only way to do it, because that is where the editors and agents are and is how we can meet them. So Sophia and I are going to put on our best dress and go. I'll have to put thought into my outfit but not right now.

I did not call Sophia back to say "yes I am going, pick me up" till just now. Yesterday Bill and I had gone to Fort Lowell pool after the mall, and while I was in the pool my Higher Self reminded me the Southwest Authors Buffet Lunch was next day and she wanted me to go. So I am going even tho I do not know why I am going.

Steve had given out an orange flyer about Southwest Authors Society at the meeting on Wednesday and as soon as I got up this morning I looked at the flyer. It gave the dates, time, and location of Buffet Luncheon. It also has other information on it. If you are a member it gives a venue to display your books to sell. Actually there are a lot of benefits to being a member. This seems to be all about belonging to the writers community in Tucson.

I had no idea Tucson even had a writers community, being a writer is such an odd thing to be. It means when you wake up you take your cup of coffee to the computer and look into your mesquite tree and watch the sparrow jumping from branch to branch and then write whatever comes into your head.

Why all the authors and editors who reject my writing when they read it, should be interested in it because they meet me at the buffet luncheon, also does not add up for me. But I am no one to talk. I had not gone back to my writing for 12 years, the whole time I lived in Tucson, till Sophia took me to the writers meeting at Barnes & Noble this past April and I went back to my writing the next day. That meeting is once a month also, and it is free. Usually by end of month I have fallen into old habits, but each time I show up at the meeting, the next morning I am back at my machine, giving writing serious whirl.

There may not be an apparent reason why showing up at Barnes & Noble at 7 pm on 3rd Wednesday of every month to listen to Steve tell us how to get published, is what got Anne back to her writing, and is what keeps Anne at it, but that is how it worked out for me.

So that is why I am not going to predict what going to the 20 dollar buffet luncheon at Plaza Hotel will bring into my life. I do not know. All I know is I am going. And at the very least I will have a story to write about it tomorrow when I wake up. And I think it may be good for me to meet editors and agents at lunch. Steve says this is how we network and we have to network. The whole concept of networking baffles me.

"What does networking mean?" I asked at the meeting

before this one.

"Meeting people" Steve said.

I'm fine with meeting people, I like to meet people. My own experience tho, is things which help me come from unexpected people in unexpected ways. It is because Katy talked to me in pool about the books she read all the time, and then would lend me the books. And when Eileen arrived in Tucson she joined the conversation. So I lent her the books Katy had lent me.

And when I xeroxed the story about swimming in the Adirondacks as a kid for my mom, a story I had written back in NYC, I made two extra copies for Eileen and Katy. That wasn't the story Eileen fell in love with, it was the other one, and she said 10 times "you have to go back to your writing Anne, I want more stuff to read."

And Sophia overheard it and told me about the writers meeting at Barnes & Noble, and day after that I was back at my writing.

It is unexpected in various ways cause Katy whose whole life is reading books and loving them so much, and because of her passion for reading I made the story for her, Eileen was just an afterthought. And Katy did not get my writing at all, she was tremendously disappointed when she read it.

It is the oddest experience I ever had to be in the midst of that 3 way conversation where Katy said to Eileen "her writing is a big nothing."

And Eileen said "no it's not, it is genre writing, genre writing is for a small limited audience who likes that kind of writing."

I didn't care what Eileen said to Katy about it because I knew she dug it. Whereas Katy was overjoyed the clutter was out of the house when I said "you can return it to me after you read it, you don't have to be stuck with it in the house."

Sophia wasn't even in any of these conversations so how she learned I was writer and got the idea to invite me to the Barnes & Noble writers meeting on how to get published I don't know. But that is what happened and is how I got back into writing.

Hahaha I guess it all came from networking at the swimming pool.

I had a great time at the Southwest Authors Luncheon

I had a great time at the Southwest Authors Luncheon. Yes Sophia was 15 minutes late to pick me up, which is ordinarily nothing, but I had dressed for it. A pretty black velvet skirt with a pattern on it, a gold scooped-neck sleeveless silk top, and a bra. It was sweltering in the house and blazing outside.

The outfit was perfect to wear for the air conditioned conference room where the meeting was held, but too hot to wear to wait outside or to lie down on bed in front of a fan. All I could do was stand at the door impatiently.

Just to kill some time I went in and left message on Sophia's machine, the message was not crabby but I was still embarrassed by it. When she arrived it was only because I wanted to undo the message that I mentioned it when I got into the car. However Sophia said she is late because she was at the funeral home, the 21 year old son of her co-worker had died, and there were so many cars she could not get out.

And I scotched that conversation instantly, I didn't want to hear the story of the 21 year old young man who had died. I was dripping with sweat, and ruining the silk blouse. I was on my way to something I didn't know why I was going there, I was very crabby. Sophia switched gears and said she leaves on September 7th for New York City to see her new grandson born last week. This is a topic I love because it is filled with joy, Sophia is ecstatic about the new baby. I really tried to be very nice to Sophia the whole rest of the ride and the whole time we were there to make it up to her being crabby in car.

I had pictured the lunch taking place in the hotel restaurant, I didn't know it would be in a conference room. Hotel restaurants in Tucson are light-filled beautiful places, atriums with plants growing, and skylights, and very fancy. A conference room is a big room with not a single window. When you arrived you line up at the desk to pay the money and get your nametag.

And the whole room was filled with big round tables, and it was filled to the brim. I was starving because I hadn't eaten a thing so I could have a lot of lunch, and I asked "when do they serve the food?" since all that was at the table was iced water and iced tea.

She said "usually pretty quickly" and I said "good."

Sophia had forgotten her notebook so I asked the man for pad of paper and pen for Sophia so she could take notes and he brought it to Sophia. I was overjoyed, I was still trying to make it up to her for being crabby in the car.

As soon as we looked into the sea of faces we saw Steve, who leads our writers group. He was at the table to the left, and he waved to both of us, and said "there are two chairs here." It was very full, maybe those were the only chairs.

When we sat down I recognized one woman and then I recognized the other. One said to me "didn't you go to Steve's writing meeting?" and I said "yes."

And then I recognized the other. I said "are you Grandma, you wrote the children's book?"

And she said "thank you for remembering."

She is the one who wrote "Stories By Grandma," and a print-on-demand company had accepted it. And she said she was going to merchandise it by sitting at the mall with her books and a sign saying "Meet Grandma."

I felt very comfortable being at the table with Steve at the center of it, Grandma on one side, and Grandma's friend from the meeting at the other side. Next to me was a woman who was slender, made up, tad glamorous with lots of make-up, and a whole lot of very fancy jewelry. She said "I am Lala, we just moved to Tucson in June from Denver when it was 110 here."

My heart went out to her instantly. On June 29th the temp went up to 113 and stayed there for a solid month. By the time the huge heat finally calmed down and went back to 108, it was monsoon season, humidity was added to the heat, that girl must think she moved to hell.

I said "it's not always like this, you will appreciate there is no winter at all, and at least you have the summer over, I moved here in November and each time someone asked 'how do you like Tucson?' and I said 'I love it,' they said 'have you spent a summer here?' and then they would scare me about the summer."

Then the MC went to the mike and the meeting started. And I thought "what about the food, I am starving." I thought "I am not going to like this one bit, having a meeting when I can't wait to eat." He opened up with two jokes. "What is the difference between a publisher and a terrorist?" Answer "You can negotiate with a terrorist." I laughed my head off, and my happiness soared.

Suddenly I realized what this is all about. We are all writers here, and we have all had our ups and downs with publishers, we are in the same boat. Everything I had been thru, they all had been thru, we had a lot in common that I had in common with no one else. Instead of being isolated people beaten down by rejection letters, we were all together having a banquet and celebrating ourselves, making merry about what we had been thru. The second joke was "How many mystery writers does it take to screw in a light bulb?" Answer, "One to write the mystery and one to give it the final twist." I loved it and I laughed my head off. I was now a perfectly happy girl.

Then he did success stories, "Anyone who has a success story in past month come up to the mike." There were only 2, one had gotten a story he wrote about an experience he had 25 years ago published in an anthology. Actually I recognized the name of that magazine, it is political. Another man, totally delighted with himself, showed us the book he just had published by print-on-demand. He was thrilled with the book and said now it is up to him to sell it himself and he will, and he hopes a real publisher will take it. I cheered both men wildly for their success. I was 100 per cent on the side of those in my own boat. I had never been with those in my own boat before.

Then the MC asked how many people are here for the first time, Sophia and I raised our hands. I didn't get to see who else did, Lala did. And when the MC said the table of invited speakers gets to line up first for the food, he said our table gets to line up second because we have the most newcomers. I was overjoyed.

On line I asked Lala what she writes. She said "suspense." She has written 4 books already and it looks like this latest one will get published, she is in negotiations.

I said "what is suspense?"

And she said "a mystery is where you don't know who did the murder, but in suspense everyone knows who did it except the main character."

I said "that is a very fine distinction."

And I pointed out "with the mystery novels written nowadays, the mystery seems to be the least of it, someone gets murdered in the first chapter and then for the whole rest of the book it doesn't figure in at all, and then in the last chapter we find out who did it, and it is always some character you didn't even remember being in the book at all, the story works just because it is fun to read."

I helped myself to salad and dressing, just two small pieces of roast beef, a nice portion of the vegetable lasagna, and six of the tiny roasted potatoes with herbs on it. They had taken away the steam tray of the hot vegetables to return it with a fresh one, so I didn't get to take any of that. I took a dinner roll with a hard crust and put butter on it. At the dessert table I took a lot of fruit. The cakes looked delicious but I thought I would wait.

When I got back to the table the man came around with coffee and I said yes. The food was scrumptious. I didn't eat my roast beef, I had taken that for the dogs. And when I had finished my food I went back to get more roast beef for the dogs. I had brought a plastic bag in my purse to slip it into.

I helped myself to another small portion of the vegetable lasagna, two slices of cantaloupe, and a piece of the lemon cake. I was actually full but the lasagna, the cantaloupe, and cake were so yummy I ate it anyway. The hot coffee was really good, I dipped my roll and butter in that. It was great meal. And then I surreptitiously slipped the roast beef into the plastic bag in my purse.

Sophia and Lala talked while we were eating. Lala told Sophia how she had arrived in June when it was 110, and Sophia said "where did you come from" and Lala said "Denver." And Lala asked Sophia where she is from. "You are not from Tucson" and Sophia said "Poland."

And Sophia told Lala that "in Polish lala means dull."

And Lala said that is not her real name. And then they talked about their children. And Sophia got to tell Lala about her brand new grandson born two weeks ago. And Lala said she can't wait to have grandchildren but it doesn't look on the agenda.

And then the meeting started up again. A woman said she is just back from New York City and she is a member of the writers union, and she will fight for us to have health care and fight for us with publishers, and the writers union is all about fighting.

I tuned her out. I am not into fighting, and my problem is not fighting with publishers, my problem is I can't find one for love or money, plus I have my Higher Self, I don't need a writers' union lawyer to fight for me. The second woman who spoke was a producer of films and Sophia is a screenwriter, I am sure she took notes, she is looking for a producer.

Then we did "new members introduce yourself." Lala told how she arrived when it was 110, and she is suspense writer, and how her new book, Sidney Sheldon in Hollywood became her friend and he is pushing it, so she thinks this one will get published. And she belonged to a wonderful writers group like this in Denver and she found this one on internet and she is overjoyed to have found it.

I was next. I said I was a writer back in New York City and I did not get published, and when I moved to Tucson 12 years ago my interests changed and I did not write, but I met Sophia at the pool and she took me to Steve's group at Barnes & Noble, and next day I went back to writing, and Steve told me and Sophia to come here, so now we are here.

Next, a man stood up and said he wanted to write a book on meditation so he made his own book, he stretched out the clothesline all thru the house and made the book. Then he gave it to his friends and relatives and they said it is boring. He showed us the book.

So then he did another book, called "How to Make a Book." He stretched the clothesline in the house even longer and made a lot of books. He showed us the book.

So then his wife got excited, and wrote a book, "All About My Life," and he stretched out the clothesline again, and showed us his wife's book. And he said "a few months ago we got a computer, that made new things possible, so now I did a book with glossy pages and color." And he showed that one.

And I cheered wildly.

And then a man stood up and said he wrote a book about a young man in the barrio, and since he is spiritual, that is also in the book. At first the young man is immature and then he matured. And I knew the story was autobiography, but the man did not say that. And I was interested to read his book.

And then a woman stood up and said she just did her book, "Illegals, Who needs them, I do." And she said how she and her husband have a 500 acre avocado farm and they could not get anyone to do the labor and the illegals came and they hired them. And not only did the illegals do the farm work, but the contractor had quit building their house, so the illegals pitched in to building their house. And it was the most glorious house in the world, with trees growing everywhere in the house and skylights. She held up her book, and said the pictures of the house are in the book. And she said how she and her husband became very close to the illegals and their families and they all helped each other.

And I swooned. I was immensely touched. What that woman said went right into my heart, I was grateful beyond measure she wrote that book.

And after that I was ready to leave. We had been there close to two hours. The MC was introducing the guest speaker of the meeting. I'm sure the guest speaker was wonderful. She was going to read from her novel and answer questions. But I had a perfect experience and I felt completed. I went into the hotel lobby to ask if I could call my husband to pick me up.

She was so nice to me. She dialed the phone number for me. Bill picked it up right away. He said "I am watching the Cardinals play."

I said "can you pick me up, I had a great time, but I don't want to stay, we can go to Robinson May and exchange your hat and I can exchange the skirt which is too big for the size smaller and then we can go swimming."

He said "I am on my way."

"I am sorry about you missing the game" I said.

He said "it's probably rerun from last night but I didn't know it was on."

I sat outside and smoked a cigarette while I was waiting for him. And then I went back inside to be in the air conditioning. The woman at the desk said "would you like bottled water" and she brought out a bottle of ice cold bottled water. I said "thank you." Just then I saw Bill drive up.

"The meeting was great" I said to Bill "it was really great, I had a wonderful time, I want to go back next month."

"Good" he said "good."

He said "I got the coach of the Wildcats to sign my hat at the scrimmage last night so now I want a new Wildcats hat, the Nike hat I bought yesterday is attractive but I want a real Wildcats hat, they are my team." So we drove to El Con mall.

I know exactly why the Southwest Authors Luncheon was great. Because it was an academy awards lunch. We, who write passionately diligently every day, and meet nothing but rejection when we send our work to publishers, awarded ourselves, we gave ourselves a banquet. Waiters came around and refilled our coffee cups. Iced tea with lemon was served to us. The most delicious chocolate cake I ever saw was set up on the dessert tray. We got to be convivial at our table. And hear from our fellows at the microphone.

This is a miraculous and blessed thing....

Samantha is back

There is a pretty bird whistle. One bird has such a pretty melodious sound. It is a pleasure to hear.

I saw Samantha yesterday at Jerry's pool. Before I moved over to swim club I had become close to Samantha. She had been Assistant Head Lifeguard and then Head Lifeguard at Fort Lowell pool when we swam there all the time before we switched to swim club. I was not close to her the way you are with a regular person because she was always up in the lifeguard stand. But when I finished my swim and Bill was still swimming I would tread water and chit-chat with Samantha up on her lifeguard stand. I guess after enough of these chit-chats an abiding affection grows.

When we came back to the public pools in mid-May I asked "is Samantha still in charge at Fort Lowell?" And I was told Samantha had taken an internship at Disney

World in Florida, but she had recently returned to Tucson, but wasn't back at Fort Lowell.

I hadn't seen her in all this time, but yesterday while I was swimming, Jerry, who is in charge of all the pools and presides over the Catalina Pool, walked out of the lifeguard room and into the supply room and with him was a young blond I recognized as Samantha.

She was in her street clothes. I called out "Samantha!" two times, but when she did not respond, I thought maybe it wasn't Samantha, but I decided to move into the first lane so I could get closer look when she got out.

When she came out I studied her and I thought "maybe it is not Samantha and that is why she did not respond," and just when I was going to keep swimming, she yelled out "Anne!" in an excited voice, it was Samantha.

Nobody has yelled out "Anne!" in an excited voice since I have been in Tucson. Working with New Yorkers and falling in love with them and being best friends with them at Disney World, had changed Samantha's personality. New Yorkers scream out your name in an excited voice when they are overjoyed to see you, but it is just not the way things are done here out West. Even tho Sam has lived in Tucson her whole life, except those 6 months in Florida with New Yorkers, it was enough.

Fourteen years in Tucson has turned this New Yorker into Tucson, and 6 months with New Yorkers turned Sam New York. We had switched places. I was just as excited to see her, but I was western low key in my expression, she wasn't. Her whole expression had turned New York City emotional. It was so much fun.

And so familiar to me. When she said, "it was time to leave, she had become so close to her New York friends, she sobbed," and she made sobbing face to go with it. Westerners don't express themselves dramatically and don't make dramatic faces to show the feeling. They say "I was really sorry to leave them" and don't make a face. They don't say "I sobbed and sobbed" and make a sobbing face.

My Samantha was transformed. Not only that, she had her long hair up in a chignon, and looked totally sophisticated— glamorous and sophisticated. Sam is a beauty but that glamour and sophistication was pure New York. I wonder if half the reason she was so delighted to see me was because it was re-link to her New York friends. Sam always knew I was a New Yorker but it wasn't real to her till she came back from Florida and left her New York friends behind.

But Sam did not like Florida. She had come back two months before her internship was done. She loved her New York friends, but could not understand why working at Disneyworld was so different from being in Tucson.

"You know how we are here in Tucson" Sam said, "I said hi to everyone, and no one said hi to me; and then I noticed in the staff cafeteria, everyone sits with the people they know, and they don't talk to anyone else, it took me a long time to figure it out." Sam described this as "culture shock." And she said she was really far away from her family. Sam is very very very close to her family. She didn't realize how far away she would be, even tho her mom visited several times.

I understood what she was saying, it is 3000 miles away, it is far distance, and psychologically too, you feel it. She was used to visiting Los Angeles and hadn't realized how different it would be. I think it was more crowded too. She said "here, there is a psychological space we all give each other, which wasn't so there."

And she was unnerved by the swamps and idea of alligators coming to get her. Altho she loves the beaches and the ocean. Because her mother had suggested she stick it out, I get the impression that when she was there, the bad overwhelmed the good, but now that she is back, all the good has risen to forefront of her mind.

"It's good you bought that 800 dollar pocketbook which was reduced to $150, you needed a classy pocketbook for back East" I said.

"I bought two more while I was there, a pink and purple one, and a brown one."

"Did you do a lot of shopping there?" I asked.

"I wanted to but I didn't have the money. I saw some really nice shoes, pink high-heels with bows, they were sooooo cute I really wanted them."

"Pink high-heels with bows!" I squealed, "O Sam they sound so cute, I guess you could have put them on your credit card."

"No I couldn't" she said, "my charge card is maxed out."

Tucson is just a way station for her now. I knew in my own bones she would stay for a while and go on to Los Angeles, that is where she really wants to go.

And she said, "I'm going to Los Angeles."

"And soon" she said.

I figure soon will be 6 months from now. She pulled up stakes and left once. Even tho it didn't work out, it was like a dress rehearsal. She is staying at her parents' house, I don't know if she will get her own place again, they are all so delighted to have Sam back and she is so delighted to be there. And she will make the same arrangement with Jerry, a leave of absence, when she does go off to California.

I knew when police academy in Tucson turned her down last summer, Samantha has a destiny. Because everything about Samantha is exactly what the police force wants. No one in this world is as calm capable and sensible as Samantha. She had been accepted by police academy and was all ready to start next day, when at the very last minute they found she had a speeding ticket in California 8 years ago, and they rejected her. It was the first time Sam was rejected for anything, she was stunned, and she was mad about it. But I knew it was destiny taking a hand, she wasn't meant to be cop in Arizona, she has another destiny.

Sam belongs in show business, she is a major talent. She does not have a show business personality, she is just incredibly talented at singing dancing acting, everything. She is an incredible performer.

Maybe it's good her New York experience in Florida, it made Sam more outgoing. She was always outgoing in a Tucson way, but now there is a NYC gloss over it. All Sam needs is to be discovered by a talent scout.

I really can't explain the NYC gloss that Sam has now, it is so subtle— but it is transforming. I would describe it as it makes Sam look more womanly. But what it is, is a heightened focus. The bird has left the nest. Sam returned from her back East experience poised on eagle wings.... and she will fly far that girl... it is her destiny…

The Girl Lifeguard at Randolph Pool

It is a sweet early morning. I saw the golden sun peeping over the mountains to the East when I went out to open the windows on the truck (and put a towel over the steering wheel) and the air is soft and pleasant.

Caren's huge green diesel truck is gone from her driveway, so I guess she has moved to Mexico. She rented a room in a friend's house in San Carlos, and rented out her room in her big Tucson house next door to us. All her other rooms are rented out too.

Now that her brother Jack has moved back to Tucson I guess he will be in charge of her house. Occasionally we see him drive up and he says hi in a very warm way. He and Bill are friends from before Caren rented out all her rooms to boarders. Back then she only rented out one room and had plenty of room for Jack to stay with her when his life turned bumpy. Bill does not think Caren will stick it out in her new life in San Carlos and will return in the Fall.

I don't know. She has a lot of plans for her new San Carlos life. She started out by renting a room, but she plans to sell real estate there, and I am sure she plans to expand from one room. She invited me and Bill to visit her there and said there is a nice bus which goes there.

If I knew Caren better I would know what precipitated this move, but I have no idea. All I know is 3 months ago she arrived at our door with huge shopping bag filled with bottles of vitamins and shampoo and conditioner and said "I am moving to Mexico, would you like this stuff?"

She told us she would be moving in mid-July, which is exactly what she did. She said San Carlos is on the beach but it is hot and humid in summer, altho nice the rest of the year. All things considered it is a stunningly adventurous thing she has done. When I see Jack next time I think I will ask him if she took her computer and if she is on email. I would like to write and ask her how things are there. I am curious about her great adventure.

Caren's great adventure is in marked contrast to my life now which seems like pure monotony. I am ashamed about the sameness of my days, and think there must be something wrong with me to live this way. And when I wake up in the morning and first open my eyes to new day, I don't know whether it's the hot stickiness on my skin or the monotony of my days, which makes me think 'O no! another day!'

It scares me this lack of enthusiasm. I think something must be wrong. But really how can I judge my life? I can observe that I am not waking up enthusiastically, but beyond that I don't know anything.

I can say it is the fault of the weather, or the fault of how I spend my time. I do not know. It could come from something else for all I know. It could be residue of feeling left from where my mind has been the whole time I have been asleep in my bed.

I can say it means I am doing everything wrong in my life, or it could mean I am going thru a purification process and I am doing what I am supposed to be doing. I don't know anything. But I jump to a lot of harsh judgments and frighten myself. And that changes my mind from lack of enthusiasm about new day, to cauldron of all kinds of upset thoughts.

Then I think maybe it doesn't mean anything at all, and

it is just mist in my mind which needs to be burned off as day starts up. And then I get scared I will project it all onto Bill and the day will be spent in tantrums about monotonous life. I guess it is best that I keep the thoughts in my own mind and deal with them there, projecting them makes them worse.

There does seem like a vast emptiness but I don't know what that means either. It could just be a big clearing out. And I don't even know what vast emptiness means. I do not know what goes into my days, how I fill my time, exactly what it is I do.

I know I read a book for part of yesterday, I think in the afternoon and evening before I went to bed. *Teacherman* by Frank McCourt. It was totally pleasant escape from my life and sometimes it was very funny, and it gave me something to think about in the swimming pool, I thought about Frank McCourt. And it inspires me about writing and makes me wonder if I should have stayed a school teacher.

Yesterday afternoon, before we went to swim pool, I dozed off while reading his book. And in the dream I met him, and I was tongue-tied. I was too shy to say anything to him, it was excruciating to even get out a few words.

Bill went to the workout gym at Randolph Pool and said "after my work-out I want to take a quick dip, so stay in the pool and I will be there in one hour."

I gamboled in the water for an hour. I don't know if what I do is called swimming. It is more like dipping into deep water and resurfacing, over and over, from one side of pool to other. I swim deep, touch bottom, and come up, then go down again, come up, half the time my legs are in the air. I like standing on my hands in the water. I did that for almost an hour. When I started to get a little bored I thought about Frank McCourt. It was interesting to have someone to think about. And I started to pick up my head a lot and look around for Bill, it was now an hour.

Then I heard the lifeguard on the stand, the beautiful girl blond lifeguard, say in a loud voice to the guy lifeguard in the water, "go into my wallet! open up the zipper! and take out all the money!"

That was such an odd thing to call out in such a loud voice. I couldn't imagine what she meant, it seemed unusual to trust someone so much to tell them to go into their wallet and take out all their money.

And then the next thing she called out in a loud voice, "I have nothing anymore! I have no boyfriend! my boyfriend cheated on me! I have no money!"

Then she called out "go into my wallet and take out my card and step on it!"

And then I heard something about wanting her money back. I had no idea what went on? Her boyfriend cheated on her and someone took her money ??? Everyone was in the water clustered around her, it was clear she was someone loved. The blond young man lifeguard loved her.

He was the one she was directing her comments to. There was a little girl who loved her too, and another lifeguard with black hair and dark skin. I came close too, I wanted to hear more. But when I arrived the topic had changed.

The little girl asked her "what does P.S. mean," and the lifeguard said "post script."

And someone said "ASAP means as soon as possible" and the little girl said "I know that."

And the beautiful blond high-up in lifeguard chair said "pps means post post script which doesn't make any sense."

And the little girl said "what does RSVP mean?"

And the blond man lifeguard in water called out "respondez s'il vous plait" in an exquisite musical French accent. I was floored. Suddenly beautiful French was spoken around me.

And then the girl lifeguard's shift was up, and she dived in the water with the blond man lifeguard and they played in the water together and I wondered if he was in love with her, it kept looking like he wanted to put his arms around her.

And then Bill arrived and I said "it is one hour and 25 minutes," and he said "I didn't know you were strict about time."

And he floated on his back, and at the other side he said "girl in gym told me Reed Park" (Randolph pool is in Reed Park) "has another pool, it is new pool, it just opened, it has tent over it."

And the man in next lane said "it is the Edith Ball Pool and it has a tent over it for people who don't want to be out in the sun."

I didn't know if I wanted to swim in a pool with tent over it, but at least it was outside. Bill said "when I come back on my bicycle to finish my work-out, I will ride over and check it out."

"Good!" I said "and get their schedule, it will be fun to find a new pool."

I had woken up at very bad odds-and-ends yesterday morning, much worse than the mere lack of enthusiasm for day today that I woke up with this morning, and a whole hour and 25 minutes swimming underwater and then moving close to hear the beautiful blond lifeguard call out "I don't have a boyfriend anymore, he cheated on me" and "go into my wallet open up the zipper and take out all my money," and hanging out in pool for another 15 minutes while Bill drifted back and forth on his back.

Somehow the whole combination had immensely soothing effect on me. Instead of my life feeling like a puzzle where all the pieces were scattered, all the pieces came back together. I guess this is called simple happiness....

My first summer camp

The night sky above the dark trees is just subtly lighter than the trees, so I guess dawn is about to break sometime soon. I can see the outline of the dark trees.

I got snail mail from my friend Basha back in New York City and when I opened it up, it was an article from the NY Times book review about Nora Ephron's new book of personal essays about her life. It was so much fun to read. I have not read anything in newsprint for so long. It was so much fun that someone had selected out something they thought you would enjoy reading, and to sit at dining table with soda on ice when I got back from swim pool and read it.

Basha and I met when we both had just turned 30. I had just started writing then. I had been writing for almost a year and I remember when we went to the Museum of

Modern Art together and had lunch in their sculpture garden, I asked Basha if she wanted to hear one of my stories. I had just written one and I wanted to try it out. I read it to her at our table in the sculpture garden.

It was about the first camp I had gone to when I was 12 years old. And the interesting thing about that camp I discovered when I wrote the story, was it had no rules, no rules at all. This didn't seem remarkable to me when I was 12 years old, it seemed utterly natural for me to be in a place with no rules at all.

It was my first time away from home, I was there for the month of July. There was even a cattle pond for swimming, the camp took place in a rundown farm in Vermont, and there were no rules about swimming either. Anyone could go to the "lake" and go for a swim by themself whenever they felt like it. There was no lifeguard.

There were no activities you had to go to. Activities were available if you wanted to go. A range of them. The girls in my bunk went to no activities. They stayed in the bunk and played Jacks. But I went to archery, I liked that. I didn't know why they stayed in the bunk and played Jacks instead of going to activities, but I knew they looked down on me for going to activities.

There was an emotional drama for me at that camp because I had only gone there because I wanted to be with Francis. My best friend from babyhood, Francis, went every single summer and raved about it all the time, and told me I had to go, it is so wonderful. And finally the summer I was 12, I asked my parents, and they said you can go for the month of July.

And my father sent off the check for 80 dollars, and duffle bag was located, and my mother wrote my name with black indelible ink on strips of fabric and sewed it on all the clothes I was taking to camp. They sent a list, two pairs of shorts, two long pants, bathing suit, two tops, etc.

And then the great day came, and my parents took me to Grand Central Station where everyone was lined up for the train taking them to camp. And we found the line for the train to take me to camp. And there was Francis. And on the train ride I sat next to her. Altho the seat was turned around so she could sit with her other friends from camp. So there was 4 of us sitting together.

And when we got there I took the top bunk above Francis. And after that Francis never spoke to me again for the rest of her life.

That train ride up to camp was the last time I sat next to

her. The great love of my life since I had been a baby, we had learned how to walk together, ended on that train ride up to camp, where I sat on one side of Francis and her best friends from camp sat on the other side.

I did not measure up.

I didn't realize it on the train ride. I was so excited and thrilled and loved every instant of what was happening around me, already I loved camp. And it took a while for it to dawn on me at camp too.

Altho as you can imagine Francis quickly changed her bed. Sairy Anne arrived and I slept above Sairy Anne, Francis moved as far away from me as she could get. She was totally embarrassed to be associated with me. I don't know how it dawned on me. I guess I would find myself alone with her, and for first time in my life find myself uncomfortable with her and tongue-tied. She was giving every impression of not liking me and not wanting to be with me. And after a while I stopped trying.

It was a new world to me, this world of the clique, and some were in it, and some were not. And clearly Francis was one of the top girls in the clique. She wasn't the leader, but she was totally accepted in it, she was part of it.

The bunk had 12 girls, not every girl was in the clique,

altho most of them came year after year like Francis. I'd guess 5 girls were in the clique, everyone else was excluded.

But that is what a pecking order is. There is the leader of the clique, the rest of the clique are her accolades. And the rest of us are nothing. I had not made the transformation to teen-ager yet. My mind was still child's mind. So I found it highly amusing I was nothing and the clique was everything. Not amused so much as interesting. I was in a new world, it was a brand new adventure, and I loved everything about my brand new adventure. That there was a clique and I was nothing, was just another interesting thing about this new adventure.

I was upset about losing Francis, and I don't think I accepted it. I accepted it that at camp she would have nothing to do with me, but I would not believe our friendship was over. I think I assumed back in the city it would return. Because I think I began a diary the following year, it only had 3 entries in it, and one of them was about Francis. I wrote "something is wrong in our friendship." I was disturbed and trying to understand it. The idea that Francis had changed her feelings for me was incomprehensible.

Because it was my very first experience of anyone changing their feelings towards me. I didn't know such a thing happened. I just assumed when you love someone you love them forever, that that is the nature of love, that the joy of your heart is always the joy of your heart.

I wasn't bothered about the clique excluding me, altho I knew it made a difference to Francis, that this is why she wouldn't talk to me at camp. I had zero feelings about the clique on my own. The idea of a clique is that they are infinitely desirable and superior to the rest of us. And there were girls in my bunk who saw them that way, and were very upset they were excluded from the clique, but I didn't get it.

"Why are you so upset?" I said.

"Because they won't let me in the clique."

"We'll just form our own clique" I said, trying to be helpful.

There were 4 of them. It was on the stairwell. They were all upset about being excluded from the clique, they were commiserating. There were tears. If they wanted to be in a clique so badly, I thought we should form our own.

But of course it upset them when I said that. Because they were so upset they were hanging out with someone who was so out of it, she didn't even know not being allowed in the clique was fate worse than death. After that even those who were excluded from the clique refused to talk to me. I was bottom of the barrel.

I could have been one with the ones unhappy about not being in the clique if only I had known I was supposed to be unhappy. So the clique stayed in the bunk instead of going to activities and played Jacks. And the ones excluded from the clique hung out on the staircase and cried. And I went to archery, and started to get good at it. I was having a ball at camp.

I even had a ball at social activities. On Friday nights there was dance at the Sugar House. It had been a working farm, that is where the maple syrup used to be made. The Friday night party at the Sugar House meant the girls would all sit on chairs next to each other, and the boys would choose which one they wanted to ask to dance. I thought this was a lot of fun.

The boys would walk up and down trying to decide who they wanted to choose. I giggled to the girl next to me "it's as if we are the candy in the candy store, and they are trying to decide which one they want." The girl moved her chair away from me. It bothered the girls not in the clique very much that they were never chosen, only the girls in the clique were chosen.

But I just thought it was a new fun game at camp, being the candy in the candy store. I could care less whether I was chosen or not, I just liked being in the game.

Of course there were great games at that camp else I would not have loved it so much. "Capture The White Flag" was an ecstasy, an adventure game in fields and woods, I loved it. And "Nose Bag Dramatics," which we played in the barn was a lot of fun too. And on "Amateur Talent Night," I was the only one from my bunk who volunteered.

I got up and threw myself all over the stage in my own interpretative modern dance. I made it up. I thought I did great. I had no idea that for "Amateur Talent Night" you were supposed to have talent, and be up there and demonstrate your talent. I thought it was for anyone who wanted to do anything on the stage.

The faces on the girls from my bunk when I finished and went back to my place were a sight. You never saw so much disgust in one place. It did not dim my enthusiasm, I overlooked it. "Why don't you get up and do something, it's fun" I told them.

When we went huckleberry picking in the field, the counselor let us take off our clothes and pick berries in our underpants. When we went to the stream to wash our clothes we were allowed to wash our clothes naked and swim in the stream. It was a great camp.

I had a great time. One night we all waited till we had been in bed, and counselors were coming around on O.D. to check on us, and then we all ran away. And I hid in the baseball field. And it was so exciting when the counselor found me and flashed his flashlight on me. I had lain there breathless in the dark when I saw the flashlight in the distance. I think that was the highest adventure of all.

Altho it was fun putting on a dress and being driven in the truck to Marlboro for a square dance. I loved square dancing.

On Visiting Day in the middle of the summer all the parents drove up from New York, and my parents drove from our summer house in Adirondacks to pick me up and take me back to Old Forge.

"I had a wonderful time at camp, next year I want to go for two months" I said. "As soon as we get back to NYC Daddy," I said, "you write out the check for two months."

Part 2

When I got back to the Adirondacks I was walking in that huge parking lot of the Enchanted Forest with my friend EllenSue and her sister Margaret one morning, and a boy on a porch wolf-whistled at me. I didn't know he meant me, until he yelled out, "hey beautiful! you in the blue jacket!"

A week later, when I was walking into town he passed me. "Hello beautiful" he said as he passed me.

I sold my soul for a wolf whistle. It was worth it. My mom's friend invited me to Inlet with her to see "Picnic" one night. There was Kim Novak with her beautiful long hair. I went into town and bought Breck shampoo and began washing my hair all the time. I went to the library to look for a book on how to be popular, all they had was how to be a model. I walked around the house with books on my head, and a clothes hanger in the back of my shirt. They said a model has perfect posture.

I received a group letter from the girls in my bunk. They said we are painting the bunk and they put splashes of the paint on the letter so I could see the color. It was a love letter. I wondered why they wrote me a love letter when I knew they all hated me.

The following year there were parties all the time because the boys were getting Bar Mitzvah-ed and there was party afterwards at the boy's house. I had a good time at the parties even tho it was at one of them I knew it was over between me and Francis.

When it neared my birthday and I saw my mom with shopping cart with big bag of potato chips, and I said "what is that there for?" and she said "never mind," I suspected there would be surprise party for me. The girls from camp were throwing surprise birthday parties for everyone.

I thought "this is not a good idea, my mother does not understand, they all hate me."

One of the boys gave me a Ricky Nelson record as my birthday present. I went into my room to play it. The boys came in with me. The girls refused to come in. They sat in the living room, looking down on me.

"Why don't you come in" I said "it's fun." They turned their sneering faces to me. I stayed in my bedroom with the boys listening to the record.

The boys were nice to me, we had fun. I had wonderful time at my surprise birthday party.

The girls never spoke to me again and never invited me to anymore parties.

One of the boys called up and invited me out on a date.

Part 3

Of course not all the girls in the bunk hated me. There was just no one who liked me. Except for Sairy Anne. She arrived a few days late, which is how Francis could get away from me. Sairy Anne slept under me. I don't remember us having conversation, there was just warm friendly feeling between us. You know when someone likes you, just as you know when someone doesn't. Because it's the opposite experience. Being near them makes you happy.

The Chinese Food Debacle, or how I learned to love the Sr 77 Blackbird

Well the Chinese take-out dinner last night was an unqualified disaster. I had a taste for Chinese food all week, so yesterday at Jerry's pool I said to Bill "can we stop at Lotus Blossom on the way home and I can get buffet to-go."

He said "OK altho his taste was for bbq chicken from supermarket."

"It's up to you" I said.

But he wanted to please me so he said "whatever you want."

"Do you want to come in?" I said when we arrived at parking lot. I thought it would be easier for me if he chose what he wanted to eat. Also there are condiments but you have to ladle them into the little plastic cups yourself, I always skip that part cause it is too much for me to do. I thought if Bill went with me he could do it.

He said "no I don't want to come in."

"OK" I said, "I'll do it myself."

He called out what he wanted, the chicken tempura.

When I arrived I knew I had come at wrong time. The dregs of lunch buffet was still there, they had not put out supper buffet, so everything in the serving trays had turned hard. I still filled up the takeout container with the chicken tempura even tho I could see it had turned hard, and then looked for other things to add. I ordered a big rice to-go with it so Bill would not have to go to the trouble of cooking rice. I helped myself to 3 egg rolls and put them on top of the rice take-out instead of in the buffet box so they would stay crispy.

There wasn't much of a selection, maybe there is no Saturday night buffet. I did manage to put the condiments in their little plastic cups. I was so proud of myself. I thought "this will be tasty dinner and a big change from what we had been eating." I ate my portion when I got home.

6 hours later at 9 pm Bill called out he is ready for his Chinese supper and sat down at the table. I realized it wasn't as easy as it seemed, because everything had to be

microwaved to make it hot again. I was a little overwhelmed at how to do it, because I realized everything would have to be microwaved separately, the rice, the egg rolls, and the dinner.

I emptied the package of rice into a big bowl, looked for a plate to put on top of it, and microwaved it for four minutes. Then I brought it out to the table. Then I took the 3 egg rolls and put them in the container the rice had come in and microwaved them for two minutes.

I brought out the condiments and the egg rolls. I made him a soda with lots of ice, and I put in the heavy package of food to microwave for 5 minutes.

He called out "come sit down Anne, I'm always halfway thru my diner by the time you sit down."

I said "I am microwaving the food for 5 minutes."

He said "that's too long, it will turn hard."

So I shut it off and brought it in. I really wanted to finish those last minute chores before I sat down at table, put the porch light on, little things. But he had said how I was always futzing around and not sitting at table when we eat.

Of course I wasn't hungry, I had already eaten when I first came home with the food. I had only planned to have a little to keep him company, an egg roll, and some other little stuff. I was making myself a glass with ice and soda when he said "sit down already!" so I turned off the microwave, brought in the food, grabbed my glass with ice and soda and sat down.

He opened up the bowl of steaming rice and said "what's this in there! don't they wash the rice! now you see why I always wash the rice!"

I don't know what he saw but he found it unappetizing and it depressed him. He carried on about it. Then he tried the chicken tempura.

"You have to be so careful with microwave" he said, "it is hard."

I said "it was hard when I got it, but I didn't know what to do, that was your order and I didn't have the wits to change when I saw it was hard."

A depressed silence fell on the table. I was actually enjoying my egg roll with the hot mustard. I had never been able to finesse getting the hot mustard before, it sure was tasty but hot. But he wasn't talking and depression was coming from somewhere.

"I didn't want to say anything Anne because I didn't want to hurt your feelings, but this food is awful, I'm not eating it, give it to Lulu," and he pushed away his plate.

I guess because he had held back his feelings all during the depressed silence because he didn't want to hurt my feelings, it now all came out in a storm.

"I am never taking you there again! I am never going to that restaurant again! I wanted fried chicken from Frys! Soup and sandwich is better than this!" We had been having soup and sandwich for past 3 nights.

He went on and on about how the food is so awful and he won't go there again.

"I am never going to that restaurant again!"

I started to get upset. Money had been spent and I am short of money now. I had put in a lot of effort at the restaurant trying to do it right. And then I had put in effort with the micro-waving.

I had been nervous at first I wouldn't be able to figure out how to microwave the 3 separate dishes and be able to serve it all without Bill having to wait at table for it.

He kept going on and on ("I had been looking forward to my Chinese dinner") and I was upset feeling like a failure. My spirits were going down. I tuned in my Higher Self who said "don't say anything" and she just sweet-talked me. The depressed silence for 15 minutes before the explosion came had been a bummer too.

I didn't want to collapse into feeling like a failure, so I just kept tuned to my Higher Self who was saying "don't say anything" and sweet-talking me to keep my spirits up.

Finally I figured he had said enough about how awful the food was. He called in Lulu so I could feed the chicken he would not eat to her. I picked out all the chicken and put it on little plate for her, and she ate it.

I said he doesn't have to tell me anymore how bad the food was, but I guess he was still saying "I will never go to that restaurant again!" when I was in the kitchen, because my Higher Self pointed out "he didn't go to the restaurant, he sat in the parking lot, if he had gone to the restaurant he could have picked out his own food and maybe it would have been better."

I really perked up when my Higher Self said that. Hearing it from him the picture was so black, I felt like I had tried so hard and everything was wrong, I had done everything wrong, altho Bill didn't blame me, he blamed the restaurant.

But my Higher Self felt there were holes in Bill's scenario. And when Bill said yet again, "I will never go to that restaurant again!" I said "you didn't go to the restaurant, you went to the parking lot."

It gave me such a lift to say that. It felt so crisp.

I went back to the table and Bill said the meal depressed him, and we sat in that depression for a while till I said "I'm going to bed" and he said "good." But instead of going to bed I came in and turned on my machine, and I posted an article about a UFO sighting in Alaska on my news site.

And the same attitude which made me say "you didn't go to the restaurant you went to the parking lot," the same refusal to let the wave of failure engulf me entirely, the same decision to just detach myself from what was happening, to refuse to be drawn into it, completely took over when I started to post.

I just decided to kick up my heels. I decided to dance and party all over my site.

My site has been dreary for long time and I had been just going along with things as they were, succumbing to the prevailing atmosphere, but when I broke free from the gloom at the table I was a new Anne. No way was I going to waltz into the gloom on my site. I kicked up my heels and danced. I was totally spirited. I made jokes about everything. I was much bolder and dauntless. It was so much fun.

Naturally when you post a UFO article there are those who come on the thread just to make jokes about it but the devil had gotten into me. When Packrat posted his joke, "I don't know why the UFO has its headlamps on, it is broad daylight," I posted back "you don't know anything about ET craft, that is its guidance system."

To my astonishment he fell for my malarkey. And came back with his own joke about flying saucers and little green men. I had a lot of jokes about that because of how the Greys do look.

Another poster who I just met (Rainsfield) posted a photo of a plane and said "this is from the '50s, we don't know what our Air Force has now."

And I posted back in all sincerity "is that a fighter jet, I don't know anything about aircraft."

And he said "it is the Sr 77 Blackbird, it is a spy plane, and it goes so fast it is top secret how fast it goes." So then naturally I had a ball posting about the Blackbird spy plane.

When nothing was happening on my UFO thread I went on other threads and cracked jokes about their posts. As much fun as I had cracking jokes with posters I am old friends with, the most fun was with the new poster (Rainsfield) I had just met on the UFO thread who told me all about the Blackbird spy plane.

He had flown one and was clearly in love with that aircraft. And for some reason all the exuberance of the new 1950s technology was translated into that plane. Seeing it in all its glory in that photo he posted, was like seeing the first of the '50s two-toned cars with fins when I was a little girl. It had the same beauty, excitement, pride, it was so alive, there was a happy spirit there. We were both astonished that an aircraft he loved so dearly had been love at first sight for me.....

I guess there's more to life than being a wife.

My Wedding and Gwen's Wedding

My whole yard is mesquite trees now. Not really, but their branches extend. So it makes greenery everywhere. They are swaying in the breeze now. Today is a lovely day. It is not as hot as it was. It dropped back down to the 80s and there is lovely breeze swaying the branches of mesquite trees and their boughs.

I lived with Bill long time before I got married. Getting married turned out to not be so easy. We went down to City Hall to get our wedding license. It was good for one month. We had to get married within the month.

But I couldn't find anyone to marry us. I went to the synagogue across the street and the rabbi didn't want to do it. So I walked up to the Catholic Church on Second

Avenue and said to the priest "my fiancé is Catholic will you marry us" and he said "no, because you are not a member of the community and some people just want a church wedding so they can have a church in their photographs."

I did not understand when he said I am not a member of the community because I was a member of the community of the Lower East Side for long time, but now I realize he meant a member of his church.

I began to get desperate because the month was almost up. I bumped into Leona in the street and told her. She is the mother of the boyfriend I had in high school. She said there is a reverend on WBAI and he has a church in midtown, she bets he would marry us.

So I called and spoke to someone. But he said he would not marry us unless we had counseling for a whole year to see if we were ready to make the big step.

I said "we have lived together for 16 years we are ready to make the big step."

So he referred me to someone else who he said might be willing to do it.

This time I knew what I was up against. So when I got on the phone with him, I began right off saying how "Bill and I had lived together for 16 years and we want to marry, we have the marriage license but Bill wants religious wedding, not City Hall, but he doesn't care which religion it is, just that it is under God."

He said "ordinarily I insist on a year of counseling to see if you are ready to make the big step but in this case I don't think you need it" and he said he would marry us on Monday.

And he gave us an address on West 57th Street, "it is near Carnegie Hall" he said.

I assumed it was one of the pretty old churches over there and I was ecstatic. The night before the wedding I set the iron on the washboard sink of my kitchen and I ironed Bill's shirt and my skirt. And Joey dropped by and I chit-chatted with Joey as I ironed. I was actually terrified about getting married but I don't know why now. It sounded like entering another world, and I didn't know what the other world would be. I guess that is why I didn't mention to Joey I was going to get married the next day. I liked everything feeling familiar and the same, Joey sitting in my kitchen saying the same stuff he always did, as if nothing had changed at all.

The reverend had said to bring two witnesses, so Ruthie

and Roberto agreed to be our witnesses and to drive us to the church for the wedding. The next morning they arrived and Ruthie was carrying a big box, "it is your wedding present." It turned out to be a beautiful Navajo blanket that Wendy had given her. Bill and I both loved it, and in fact it is one of the few things we took to Tucson. It is up on the wall of our living room now.

Bill and I were both in terror of getting married, altho we both tried to hide it from Ruthie and Roberto and from each other, and acted like everything was normal. It was Martin Luther King Day so Bill was off work. Ruthie had just had 3 weddings to Roberto over the last few months, so she was old hand at getting married.

She had met Roberto in Venezuela the year before, they had married there at a civil wedding, then again at religious wedding because that is what Roberto's mom wanted, then Ruthie's mom threw big fancy catered Jewish wedding for Ruthie and Roberto in Roslyn Long Island, a fancy suburb of NYC.

Roberto had only been in USA for one month so I gave directions on how to arrive at Carnegie Hall. The address was a block or two west of that, on the north side of the street.

"OK we are at Carnegie Hall now Roberto, we just have to keep our eyes peeled for a church now on the other side of the street."

We arrived at the address but it was not a church. It was just an office building and when we walked in and took elevator to our floor, it turned out it was a center for disturbed adolescents. We went to the desk and I asked for the name of the reverend, and she directed us to his office. It turned out he was a counselor for the disturbed adolescents there. I was crestfallen. That is not how I pictured my wedding being.

But Bill had sat in the chair in the waiting room, reading the brochure about the center, and told me "this is a place where they try to help teenagers." He was overjoyed about it. The fact that Bill liked it so much reassured me.

I knew we were in a shrink's office and I tried not to say to myself "my wedding is taking place in a shrink's office." He arrived and enthusiastically greeted Ruthie and Roberto, and the three of them had enthusiastic vivid chat. I thought Bill and I are 'sposed to be the stars at our own wedding, but in fact we were both so nervous neither one of us could open up our mouth. Then he said "join hands" and I was trembling all over and it helped me to put my hand in Bill's hand, it steadied me.

I was not crazy about the wedding ceremony he wrote. It was not one bit like the movies. There was poem by Tagore, and something from an Apache wedding ceremony. I would have loved it that it was Apache, maybe like everyone I always identified with the Native Americans, but it was all about big spaces in the relationship and big spaces are good. And Bill and I had just gone thru 3 such stormy years we were not close at all. I didn't want big spaces, I wanted to be close again.

Altho I will say, after the 3 tumultuous years of storminess in our relationship it was tremendously meaningful to be standing up there marrying him. For us to be standing there hand-in-hand, being married, in front of witnesses. I experienced the depth and reality of my love for Bill. It had withstood all the storms.

After the wedding we signed the papers. And Ruthie and Roberto again chatted it up with our minister, and again Bill and I said nothing. Then Bill and I took Ruthie and Roberto out to lunch at small Italian lunch place in our neighborhood.

I changed out of my wedding clothes to be more comfortable. I had forgotten what I wore to my wedding, but when I was cleaning my room this past September I found an envelope on top of the closet which contained the wedding photos Ruthie had taken. I had worn a white silk blouse with short puffed sleeves, creamy white, a blue cotton ruffled skirt from India, because you're sposed to wear something blue at your wedding.

And for some reason black very sexy stockings that you'd imagine a prostitute wearing, and I assume sexy shoes altho those were not in the photo. I have no idea why I wore those black very sexy stockings. It makes for an unusual wedding pic. There is my black black hair, that white blouse, that robins egg blue long ruffled skirt, and then because I am sitting down and pulled up the skirt to my knees those black stockings. Ruthie lent me her wedding ring for the part in the wedding where Bill puts the ring on my finger, so I guess that was the borrowed part. Also there is crimson nail polish on my finger nails. I look like Snow White.

I put together the outfit the night before. I didn't want to wear my wedding outfit for going out to lunch because it had been such big deal to be married, I was in state of shock, I thought it would help me feel normal again to change into an ordinary dress. Ruthie brought me a black dress made of cotton, very simple and comfortable, but by a designer so it was pretty and I liked it and I changed into that in the adolescent help center girls bathroom.

It had rained all the way in the car to our wedding and on the way back to Lower East Side, huge and loud hail kept hitting windshield. I loved it because I knew it was Heaven throwing rice at our wedding. I knew it was a blessed wedding.

We went to our favorite Italian lunch place, just simple tables in one small simple room, and Bill went next door to buy a bottle of wine and we all had lunch and I was happy but I was still in shock. The next day Bill's boss offered him the day off because "you just got married."

"Take the week off" he said.

Bill said "are you kidding, I am in a state of shock, I want to come back to work to feel normal again."

So the following year when Gwen called me up to say she and Phil are going to get married I wanted to save her the trouble I went thru.

"Just call the Unitarian Church, they will be willing to marry you without making you wait a year, tell them how long you and Phil have lived together, and don't let them put in the part about huge spaces in your relationship."

Two weeks later we arrived for the wedding. It was held in the loft of Phil's daughter in the West Village. Instead of my minister there was a woman minister. And all of Gwen and Phil's friends and relatives from the Dojo were there. From karate school, aikido school, tai chi, and from when Gwen had worked at the print shop. It was before she became a beautician.

Everyone was gathered and the lady minister was there, but there was a hold-up.

"What is the hold-up?" I asked someone.

"Gwen refuses to arrive" I was told.

Phil was already there with the minister with his son standing next to him as best man.

So I went downstairs and there was Gwen.

"I refuse to go" she said, "everyone is sitting there staring, it is scaring me."

I said "nobody is sitting there staring, they are all talking to each other, come on up, no one will even notice you arrive, I have been chatting with Linda F's best friend from the print shop, I am so happy to meet her."

"Are you sure no one will notice me?" she said.

"No one will notice you they are all talking to each other."

It was big fat lie, but what could I do. Gwen had to show up at her own wedding.

"We'll go up together and I'll go up front with you."

"Stay with me" she said.

"I will."

I swear I must be a crack pot. We walked up the stairs, I said to everyone "Gwen is here, no one look" and we walked up to the front together.

Then Gwen put her hand in Phil's and I knew she was fine and I took a seat. Gwen and Phil had worked with the lady minister to say what they wanted her to say so it was a lovely ceremony, and Gwen was happy afterwards.

"You didn't tell me the truth, Anne" Gwen said afterwards.

"I know but what could I do" I said.

I sat with Gwen and her friends from the print shop and we chatted.

Then Bill and I walked home across town.

The French Are Very Nice

Bastille Day. I guess back in New York City Lisette is on her way right now to drink a glass of champagne at the French embassy. Bruno met Lisette when she was an au pair girl in New York. I think his friend was dating a French girl and she brought along Lisette, and Bruno met her, and they have been together ever since. Lisette has very short hair but she had worn a fall on her date and Bruno was attracted to her long hair.

Lisette was actually born on a houseboat on the Seine but her father went to Heaven early in World War 2, and Lisette and her sister and her mother lived in factory district of Paris. I think Lisette's first job was one of the seamstresses for the couturier house in Paris.

She didn't want to live in France anymore, she could not make up her mind between Switzerland or USA, but she got job as au pair girl here in USA and came to New York City. Where she met Bruno.

Bruno is Italian from Brooklyn and grew up in Canarsie. His father was a mechanic and owned a garage, and of course Bruno planned to be a great mechanic too and work in the garage. He has sisters and brothers. He did not get high enough grades to matriculate at Brooklyn College so he had to go to Night School. Altho I think he registered at day school anyway, and went to school there, till they caught up with him and made him go to night school.

I am surprised now, when I look at it, how little I know of each of theirs background, I thought I knew it so well. I would take my dog to Tompkins Square Park in the mornings and if Bruno was there with his dog, I'd walk around the park with Bruno; if Lisette was there with the dog, I'd walk around with Lisette. Whatever I learned was from the chit-chats on these walks. I thought I knew so much, but now I see I don't know anything. I think Lisette wanted a parrot and she wanted a dog and her mother said "when you are grown up and have your own apartment you can have both of them."

Altho Lisette does not seem emotional she is more emotional than she seems. When she took her dog to East

River Park, she got into argument with a German girl there. I don't know what the argument was about, maybe her dog, but Lisette got mad and upset and at the end she yelled at the girl "you killed my father."

And when Margaret Thatcher came over from England to meet with Reagan, and Bruno said complimentary things about her, "Nancy is so scrawny, you could tell Reagan liked putting his arms around Margaret Thatcher"—Lisette's whole comment on it was, "we French have not forgotten what the English did to Jeanne d'Arc." She was still mad about it.

Mainly I was involved hearing about Lisette's current life. She was a happy girl. She had her bicycle and went everywhere on her bicycle. She decided to go back to school. You can't go to college unless you are able to pass a math test, so Bruno set out to teach Lisette math. She had a math block. I never understood what a block was, until I tried to teach Lisette something she wasn't able to get, as we were walking our dogs. It was something simple and obvious, but her mind froze up and she couldn't see it. I broke it down into its simplest parts, until the question was practically "what is one plus one?" When Lisette answered "minus one" I knew she had math block and I gave up.

But the girl has persistence, and next thing I knew she was taking college courses. Her first assignment was to write a biography. Her French accent was so thick, there was no way I could figure out the word she was saying was biography. I tried a few times to figure out the word but gave up. So then she continued, "I wrote a biography of the bicycle, did you know the bicycle was invented by the French." Lisette loved college. Her majors were French, and American Literature.

We had a tiny contretemps once. On our walks she would complain the whole walk, how America is bad and France is better. One day she said "in France if you speak French poorly they will correct you. But" she said "here, no one corrects me on my English."

I was surprised that was one of her complaints, here in America we consider it rude to correct someone's pronunciation, but she made it clear that is what she wanted. So the next time she pronounced a word which was unrecognizable in English, I corrected her pronunciation. And she was furious. I knew it was a rude thing to do.

Because of her accent I couldn't get every word she said in sentence but enough words to understand what she was saying. Most of her mistakes were charming. When the park police were giving us all tickets for dog-off-the-leash, Lisette said "Anne! watch out! they are here! they are all on their talkie-walkies."

Bruno could not speak a word of French and when Lisette's sister called from France, since she could not speak English and Bruno could not speak French, they were unable to say one word to each other. One time Bruno's mother came to visit, and his brother came to protect his mom. Bruno said his brother brought his gun.

Our neighborhood was bad neighborhood then, altho now I hear it is fancy-schmancy. Bruno had bought a building when the neighborhood was an atrocious dangerous slum. He bought the building for idealistic purposes. Bruno is an idealist. He planned to sell the apartments for $200 each, 1/3 to Puerto Ricans, 1/3 to blacks, and 1/3 to whites, which is maybe what he did. Those little apartments are co-ops. He kept two of the tiny apartments for him and Lisette, one above the other.

And of course Lisette decorated the apartment as if she lived in Paris, she washed her windows till they were sparkling and put white lace curtains on them.

Bruno got nothing but grief from his idealistic

adventure. When one of the Puerto Ricans was sent to jail, he told Bruno "if you touch my stuff I'll kill you when I get out." He never paid any of the money he was supposed to pay. They did have meetings about things which needed to be bought or done to the building, and the meetings were always acrimonious. Bruno is the mildest of all people, I never heard him raise his voice, but he is stubborn. It is from Lisette I learned how stubborn Sicilians are.

I think when I met Bruno he was already going to graduate school at the New School. When he finished he looked for a job. It was the middle of steamy New York City summer during a heat wave, and Lisette said, "it is so silly he is wearing his 3 piece suit." And sure enough there was Bruno, in woolen jacket, vest, and pants, coming from a job interview. The book on how-to-find-a-job had said "wear a 3 piece suit."

Bruno eventually landed a job which drove him crazy. His job was the identical experience of being driven crazy by all the fellow cooperators in his building. It was some project funded by the City to help people in the Bronx, but everyone on the job and everyone involved drove each other crazy. When Bruno couldn't take it anymore, he switched jobs, to another job which drove him crazy.

It was the same kind of deal, but this time for the Orthodox in Brooklyn. The rabbi drove Bruno crazy, ditto the rabbi's daughter. Obviously that is what Bruno likes, he likes all these ins and outs of people relationships, and being driven crazy.

And coming up with ideas of how to manipulate them to do what he wants, just as he does with his fellow cooperators. Bruno uses manipulation to get what he wants but for good purposes not bad purposes, to carry out his idealist vision for everyone's best interests. I will say that for Bruno, he always has his eye on the ball, he is single focused in accomplishing whatever good he is determined to accomplish.

"Maybe you are the reincarnation of Machiavelli" I told him one day when we were walking our dogs, when he went over with me another strategy he was using so things could be accomplished.

All of this was meat and drink to Bruno but Lisette was the opposite. Her life was completely simple and straight-forward. She loved nature, and even tho you'd think Manhattan doesn't have any nature, Lisette found it wherever she went. When Bruno and Lisette visited us in Tucson she told me how she had seen a dove in Central

Park. And when we walked around Tompkins Square Park, I would always hear about the nature she had seen.

Because my neighbor was French, Lisette would come and visit my neighbor and then drop in on me. Lisette and Simone were not the same. Simone loves clothes, perfume, lipstick, and jewelry. Simone is the one who told me, "all a woman needs to wear, Anne, is lipstick and earrings, that brings sparkle to her face." So I decided to buy a lipstick. I told Lisette, but Lisette said "why should I wear lipstick, who am I going to kiss!" She scoffed.

Lisette wore no make-up and only wore simple clothes, good for riding a bike.

Simone's background was different. She actually grew up in Morocco because her father was assigned to NATO there, and her parents were always attending balls and dinners at the French ambassador's mansion in Morocco. But Simone and Lisette liked each other even tho they were so different.

I have to say based on my two experiences of getting to know French people up close and personal the French are very nice.

Jane

Jane Pollack's birthday was yesterday. You remember for a long time the birthday of your best friend when you are little girl. She was year behind me in school cause cut-off date was April 30th and I was born at start of April, Jane was born 2 and a half months later on June 23rd.

I had an earlier best friend, Debbie Bernstein before I started school, when we still lived in Manhattan. But that is further away in my mind. I see the passionate little girls arrive with their moms at my swim club and their passionate friends, and their new baby brother just born, and how the whole world revolves around Madeline, Madeline is one of the little girls, and I know that was me back in the days when Debbie was my best friend. It is the world before school, you spend much more time with your mother.

By the time of Jane I was in 3rd grade, Jane was in 2nd grade, and we were best friends. She lived in the apartment above mine. I was in 3F and she was in 4F. It would take a writer with far more talent than I have to do justice to Jane because there is nothing to say about her. She is the salt of the earth and she is bland.

It may have to do with times. Maybe there is a time from ages 8 to 12 when your whole focus is on your skills, your games. Jane and I played with each other but what we played were games. We played Jacks with each other, we played cards with each other, we played board games with each other, and outside we played in groups. We played chinese handball, regular handball, punch ball, stickball, and jump rope, also Potsy and Girls & Boys.

Also Jane and I did things together. We traveled by train to Rochester to visit my grandfather. We traveled by subway to Lower East Side to take modern dance classes. We traveled by bus to Jamaica to take ballet. We went to the movies together. We rode our bikes together along with two other girls. We took the subway to her dad's office on Fulton Street where he sold jewelry.

We went to Woolworth's together for sodas. And had lunch at the Woolworth's in Jamaica.

We were together a lot. And the friendship lasted till I was about 15 because I remember Jane looking out my window when my cousin Richie arrived for Thanksgiving when I was 14 and saying "your cousin Richie is good looking."

He had just bloomed into his good looks as I had bloomed into mine. And I was in high school then. And the June before high school when I was 14 and few months, Jane and I were together in my room when Jane espied my date arriving to take me to the prom. So we did continue to hang out together even when the time of games was over.

But she was central in my life during the time of games. Every Friday night when her dad returned home from the city he bought Jane a new board game, and we played with them. That is how I discovered "Go To The Head Of The Class" a game I loved. Also Jane taught me "Candyland," a board game she had already had. The only board game I had was "Monopoly" but Jane also had wonderful game, "Chutes and Ladders." O I also had "Clue" but Jane had all the games. "Chutes and Ladders" was a lot of fun and I think there was a game called "Sorry" too.

We played board games until we both discovered Jacks. Then all we played was Jacks. But somehow there was always a lot of cards. Jane and I learned card tricks together and played them. We played "Double Solitaire." Jane taught me "Knucks." I guess our big game was "Rummy" which we played endlessly. If Myrna and Carol were also there we played Poker. Jane and I were well matched, we competed.

In June they put up the sprinklers in the kiddie playground behind our building, the playground we all played in, and Jane and I got into our bathing suits and went under it. Also when Jane's parents took Jane and Amy, her little sister, to visit their friends or relatives on Long Island who had a sprinkler, I was invited to go under their sprinkler too.

And when my parents took me and Jimmy, my kid brother, to Jones Beach, Jane was invited to go into the ocean too. I remember Jane being with me at Jones Beach because after we had finished swimming and wanted to go back in the water Jane and I both went in in our underpants, that was fun.

And amazingly one summer, while we were up in the Adirondacks, Jane's family came and spent a week on 4th Lake. It was a country club at Rocky Point, but I guess they rented a cabin. I remember being excited when we got in the car to drive Route 28, a winding road thru the mountains to 4th Lake, and I could see Jane.

I had my own friends in the mountains. But returning back to NYC and seeing my NYC friends was always big thrill at first. I would get out of the car and rush to Jane's apartment. And Jane's mother, Gert, would water my mother's plants for us when we were gone.

On the other side of the building was Sheila, and Jane and Sheila were also best friends, and Gert was best friends with Sheila's mother Frieda. I really have no idea how Jane and Sheila played together, they seemed so different to me.

I would play with Sheila after school cause she and I were in the same class and our way of playing was so different than what I did with Jane. We didn't play games. Sheila introduced me to her books. She had the "Honeybunch" books and then the "Bobsey Twins" books and I borrowed all of them from her. Then we would watch "Hit Parade." Sheila introduced me to "Hit Parade." And Sheila had sheet music. These were the songs which were on Hit Parade. It had the words and I guess the notes. Sheila would sing "Dance With Me, Henry" and I would sing along with her.

In Sheila's room we would play "school." Sheila never

played outside with us. She didn't join us for chinese handball or punch ball or jump rope. Sheila did not have a bicycle, she did not learn how to roller skate. That was another big thing Jane and I did. We roller skated at the school playground, or around the buildings, and thru the driveways. We got my mother to take us to the rink, where we ice skated and roller skated both.

So it's a mystery to me what Jane did when she went over to Sheila's room to play. Altho when we were all in the playground and the mothers were sitting on the benches we heard Sheila screech out the window "Jane is eating raw hamburger meat." I guess Sheila was telling her mother this. Jane always liked to eat and so did I. We spent a lot of time eating together.

Jane had tv before we did so we spent a lot of time also on the living room rug in front of her tv. That was how I discovered "Father Knows Best." Jane discovered it and I watched it there. It was thrilling at first. I watched it with her every week.

I watched tv with Sheila at Sheila's house too but the programs she liked were grown-up shows. We would watch Sid Caesar and Imogene Coca. At Jane's house we watched Superman.

In the dining car on the way to Rochester Jane and I ordered a jelly omelet. It was the first time I ever tasted that, I liked it. And when we got to Rochester we turned on my grandpa's tv and watched "Kukla, Fran and Ollie," I had never seen that either.

When someone is your companion in play you mainly remember them at play, not that much catches your notice about them. I noticed when my dad gave us arithmetic problems to solve in the car as game when he was driving us somewhere, Jane was very good at arithmetic, even better than me.

And I was surprised when I learned "Knucks" from Jane because it is cruel game, Jane was never cruel. And I remember the smell of her father's garage, when we would go over there to unlock it so Jane could get her bike. My bike was in the bike room downstairs of our building.

All I can think is Jane must have been incredibly easy going if we never once conflicted, or rubbed against each other. Her habits were different from mine. When I got something new to wear I wore it right away but Jane liked to save it in its original plastic and keep it in her drawer and show it to me in her drawer. As soon as I saw her pretty new sweater sets in plastic in her drawer I wanted my sweaterset in plastic too. I was the same as my dog now is about his bone. As soon as I give him one he rushes into yard to bury it, but then he wants one to eat also. I wanted to wear my new clothes and save them all pristine in my drawer too.

I got to see Sheila once when she blossomed into lovely young woman. I was coming home on bus when I was halfway thru college, or perhaps it was only my 2nd year, and to my astonishment the glamorous girl with all the make-up on and looking very pretty was Sheila. She told me she was secretary in Manhattan and I was astounded at her salary. Sheila was very smart, smarter than me. We had been in the accelerated class together in junior high but I could not keep up and Sheila had no problem.

I guess I played more in Jane's house than she did in mine because she had the board games, she had the tv. We did play Jacks on the linoleum in my foyer, but we played a great great great deal of Jacks in her bathroom. Her apartment had wall-to-wall carpet everywhere except in kitchen and bathroom, so we squeezed into that tiny bathroom, just enuf room for two little girls to squeeze, next to the clothes hamper under sink, and played endless Jacks there. We learned how to do Backsies there and how to do Fancies, Cherry-in-the-basket and Jack-be-nimble. And of course endless card games on the rug. For "Double Solitaire" it's possible we needed two decks of cards.

She had a cousin Harriet who was a few years older than us, who lived in Building 5, and sometimes we would visit her cousin Harriet and her cousin Harriet would come over. And of course half the time Myrna and Carol joined us for play, there were 4 of us playing Jacks on my mom's foyer linoleum, or 4 of us playing Poker at Carol's dinette table. Myrna and I did conflict, there were fights, and then Myrna would put a note in the empty milk bottle outside my door saying "let's make up" and we would.

That is why I don't understand, in all our furious competition, all our games, all our closeness, all our long afternoons together, how it is possible we never conflicted. Not about Jane, who could conflict with her? She was perfectly easy-going nice girl. But look at me! But maybe just as Jane and I were perfectly matched in every single game we played, I guess it's possible we were perfectly matched as friends too.

She had that warm easy-going nature, in astrology she is probably Taurus, that lovely sweetness of a cow, akin to placid. Jane was unruffled and unruffleable. And she was rooted as a tree. She never objected to me. Because altho I never attempted to budge Jane, I am sure she would have been unbudgeable. So even tho all our games were outdoor games of action or indoor games of mental or physical concentration, it's like those lovely fields you pass in New York State, the contentment of the cows outside, and deep shelter shade trees over them.

For 3 and a half years I spent all my free time with Jane, or most of it, playing with Jane, and it was an instant which stretched into eternity. Because Jane provided the sweet cowy contentment and the sheltering shade of tree. We lived in apartment building projects surrounded by more apartment building projects somewhere out in Queens. Both our dads worked in Manhattan. But for Jane, who was daughter of Mother Earth herself, extended all the sweet graciousness of our lovely Planet to us. All that is sweet and warm and nurturing came from Jane. It was blessed friendship.

Mary Wilner

I dreamt about Mary Wilner last night. In my dream I was so happy to see her. She looked beautiful. I was overjoyed to see her and be with her. There were other people there, and I introduced them all to Mary. I said she was my best friend. I couldn't remember whether I was 7 or 8, I decided on 8, "she was my best friend when I was 8, she came to my 8 year old birthday party, we used to ice skate together," I told everyone. "We had pompoms on our figure skates" I told someone.

In the dream the photo of Mary in my scrapbook, at my 9 year old birthday party, Mary and my other 3 best friends all together, was clear in front of my eyes. Mary in the middle, so vivid. In fact I don't remember who else was in the photo, for me it was always Mary. I guess the other girls were the girls in my building, who I played with all the time. Playing with Mary was special, she did not live where I lived.

Now that I am awake, and remembering my dream, but also remembering Mary and our friendship, everything is the same as it was in the dream. I still don't quite remember whether I was 7 or 8 when we first became best friends, but I would still go for 8. I can still see that photo in my scrapbook in front of my eyes.

Everything is the same, except for the pompoms on our ice skates. That is true, we both had those big red wool pompoms on our ice skates that we made ourselves. However I remembered that in my dream, I wouldn't have remembered it now if it had not been in my dream.

I had bought the photo album at Saks 5th Avenue when I was in my mid-twenties. Never in my whole entire life would I have bought an expensive fancy leather photo album at Saks 5th Avenue, if I had not been stoned on pot.

I have no idea now why I was walking along 5th Avenue stoned on pot. It was not something I typically did. Either I stayed in the house when I was stoned, and thought about astrology, and made diagrams to help me, or I walked along the streets of my own neighborhood, the East Village.

I did not take the subway up to 57th Street and stroll along 5th Avenue. However I was strolling along 5th Avenue stoned on pot, and I did walk into Saks Fifth Avenue stoned, a very expensive store I had never been in. And on one of the first counters where you enter, was this black leather very expensive photo album, and I liked it and I bought it.

It was completely out of the usual for me, because all I spent money on was clothes. If I had decided I wanted a photo album I would have gone to Woolworth's and bought a cheapie one. But I had never wanted a photo album, all my photos were stuffed at the bottom of the bottom drawer of my dresser.

Of course having made this extravagant purchase, I came home, got out all my photos, and placed them in the album. It was huge, leather-padded, luxurious and fancy. Oddly enough, looking back on it, I think it was one of the best purchases I ever made. I never would have had the incentive to actually put all my photos in an album, if I had just bought a cheapie one from Woolworth's, but of course with Saks Fifth Avenue photo album, you put all your pictures in right away. You use it. And it displayed them all beautifully and kept them safe.

And for a long time I had the joy, whenever I wanted to look at the photos, of getting out the beautiful album, and looking at all the photos, put in with care, and nicely set up there.

And that is where I always saw the photo of Mary at my 8th birthday party. My dad took the photo. He took all the photos in my album. He was an amateur photographer and loved to photograph. He was also a brilliant photographer, all the photos were filled with life. He always had his camera with him, so it was more than pics at my birthday party.

After I played punchball or stickball with my friends Myrna, Jane, and Carol, in the tiny little park behind my building, I guess on weekends my mom would send down sandwiches for all of us. We'd sit on the little bench and eat them.

How my father happened to be there with his camera one time I don't know, maybe he brought down the sandwiches. The photo wouldn't mean anything to anyone else, 4 little girls bent over their sandwiches, in their punchball playing clothes.

My friend Diane sitting next to us in the dress she always wore, I have no idea why her mom dressed her in dresses, it meant she never played any rough and tumble games with us, maybe she was "steady ender" if we played jump rope.

Also at the end was my brother, because he hung around with us when he wasn't playing with his own friends. It is a good snapshot because it captures our whole life of play back then, altho all we are doing is eating our sandwiches.

But for me, I looked at the photo and see our whole life of play in that tiny little playground, where we played Chinese Handball for hours on end, Asses Up at the end of Chinese Handball, punch ball, stick ball, and Skelsy, also Catcher Flies Up.

The end of the photo album was as unexpected as its beginning. I bought it on impulse stoned on 5th Avenue, it was one of the very few things I took with me to Tucson. 6 months after we moved to Tucson I found *A Course In Miracles* in the public library here and began reading it.

After renewing it 4 times I bought it, it became my whole life. It took me a whole year to read the 1000 page Text, and then another year to do the 365 Lessons in the Workbook, one lesson a day was the rule. After I finished the Text and before I started the Workbook, I was completely convinced of what he was teaching, that the past doesn't exist, that the past never happened.

I really wanted to believe that because there had been troubles in the years before we left NYC for Tucson, and the idea that the troubles could be gotten rid of, and replaced with a clean slate, was all I wanted with all my heart. I decided to take my precious photo album with all my precious photos and throw it in the garbage can outside, to be taken to the dump.

It took a lot for me to do that because I loved the album. I loved the photos my father had taken. There were photos in there before memory really began for me, of me and my best friend Hannah on the swings on Old Forge beach.

And beautiful photos of my father and mother, so young and beautiful, when they visited Miami before I was born.

Photos of me and my first best friend Francis in our snowsuits, she had that pink pretty woolen coat with leggings, in Central Park and Riverside Drive, and even one of me kissing her.

And one of my father giving me my bottle, you don't see me, just my father, dressed so nicely leaning over the beautiful high English carriage he had bought my mom when I was born, so it would be easy on her back.

There is Leon on Riverside Drive leaning over the beautiful carriage, and maybe you see the bottle. I am not sure if you see baby Annie, my mother took the photo and she does not have my father's flair for composition.

But I was adamant. Believing what he said in *A Course In Miracles* was my salvation, my way out. I wanted more than anything else in the world for the past to not have happened, and to have all my recent troubles disappear. I wanted fresh new sparkling clean slate, a present with no past. I couldn't think of any way to put my money where my mouth was, but to consign my beautiful photo album to the garbage dump. And I did it. I felt like acting on it I would make it happen.

I met Mary because both our moms sent us to the same Shula in Forest Park. I don't know why my mom sent me to that Shula. The reason she gave me, "I want you to know that there are other parents who think the way me and daddy do," may be the real reason, or may be not.

I guess I did ask my mom the reason for everything she did. Altho that surprises me now. I have no memory of ever asking her "why?" about anything, except for the time when she refused to let me go back to Old Forge Catholic

Church summer school when I was 4 years old and I really really really wanted to go back.

"Why can't I go!" I kept saying, "why can't I go!"

"Because we're Jewish, that's a different religion," she kept saying.

"So what!" I said, "so what!" I said.

"We're Jewish it's a different religion" she kept saying.

I didn't understand her answer but she wouldn't back down, I was not allowed back. I have no memory of ever asking her "why?" about anything else, unless it was something I wanted with all my heart, she wouldn't let me have it, "why can't I have it?"

Maybe I asked "why do I have to go to Shula on Sunday mornings?" (Shula is Jewish Sunday school, I went to school all week, I liked having Saturday and Sunday just for play.)

And she said "because I want you to see that daddy and I are not the only people who think the way we do."

My parents were socialists, and she was right, no one in my class and no one in my building, their parents were not like my parents, they did not spend the weekends giving out leaflets, or standing on the corner collecting signatures to petitions. And I knew my parents' ideas were different from the ideas of other parents, because I was warned repeatedly not to say a word to anyone (it was the McCarthy era).

But I had zero desire to give up playing on Sunday mornings to go to Jewish school in order to find out other kids had parents like mine. I accepted my parents were different. It seemed normal to me my parents were different. And in fact it wasn't their ideas that bothered me (the difference in their ideas). What embarrassed me is they went bicycle riding with their tennis racquets to Kissena Park on the High Holy Days, when everyone else's parents stood on the corner in their fanciest clothes and women wore their mink stoles.

I guess I thought if my parents were not going to observe the High Holy Days, and I didn't think there was any reason why they should, they should not embarrass me by letting everyone (I guess by this I meant my friends) see them in their Bermuda shorts either. They should stand on the street corner too, in a mink stole which she did not possess, and join the discussion about how not one drop of food went down their mouth all day.

Which wasn't true of course. My mother had served us all the same breakfast she always served when it wasn't a school day, pork sausages and scrambled eggs, orange juice and toast and cream cheese. I had no problem that our family ate this when you're not supposed to touch food or water, but it should be a secret, and my mother and father should put on their fanciest clothes and stand on the corner with everyone else and say how they did not eat a thing. And if they weren't going to do that, they should hide out, not parade on their bicycle with their tennis racquet as they took off for Kissena Park.

Maybe my mother sent me to Shula because she had been sent to Shula as a kid in Rochester. Her father was a socialist. I don't know if her big brother and big sister were sent to Shula, but little Eleanor was. Her grandfather (not a socialist) had a Hebrew School (to prepare boys for their Bar Mitzvah) and Gus and Annie were sent to that. But baby Eleanor was too little for Grandpa's Hebrew School, so maybe when she got older, her dad sent her to Shula instead.

The Shula I was sent to was in the area of Forest Park, so we drove thru the endless most beautiful park in the world. That drive was incredible. It went on forever. In Autumn the leaves were all changing, I never experienced so much beauty, I loved that drive. I guess during the week it was a private school in Queens, and they rented it out on Sundays for the Shula.

We sat in one of their classrooms, maybe it was a kindergarten classroom, we sat on such little chairs, and the toys were all around in cubbies colorfully painted. And the woman in charge of the Shula hung out in the principal's office, Miriam. However her son always acted up in Shula, so she had to come into our room and tell her son to stop acting up, but he refused to stop acting up.

Irving would sit at the head of the table, they pushed all the little tables together, so we sat around it, with Irving at the head and he taught us Jewish history. Then he got up and Martin sat down and we were taught how to read and write Yiddish.

Jewish history was interesting. It turns out that everyone was always trying to kill all the Jews. So all the stories were how about first— they were all strange names, interchangeable in my mind— first the Assyrians tried to kill all the Jews, but the Jews saved themselves, then the Babylonians tried to kill all the Jews, but they saved themselves. The names were all like that.

The only story which was interesting, even tho the theme was identical to the rest, was the Purim story, because that featured a beautiful young woman, which is the only thing which interested me. Her name was Esther, which of course resonated for me because of my aunt Esther, and there was a beauty contest and the king chose her to be queen and she was Jewish, so of course when they tried to kill the Jews again, beautiful Queen Esther saved the Jews. Remarkably it made no impression on me that everyone was always trying to kill the Jews, that that is what Jewish history is, I could care less, I only cared about how beautiful Queen Esther was.

Then Martin came in and we got out our notebooks and first we learned how to say the alphabet in Yiddish, and we learned how to say "ich bin a maidel, du bist a yingel" (I am a girl, you are a boy). And we learned the Yiddish word for notebook, and for pen, and for read. And we learned how to write in Yiddish "I write with my pen, I write in my notebook, I read my book." And that is all we learned.

We didn't spend much time learning during the reading and writing Yiddish class because of Miriam's son acting up. That was very dramatic and took up a lot of time. And culminated with Martin going to the principal's office and bringing in Miriam. Who would yell at her son to stop acting up, and he wasn't afraid of his mother, and he acted up more while she was yelling at him.

However as a result of all this my mother found out Miriam's husband was an optometrist, so when I could not read the bottom two lines of the eye chart in 6th grade "line up to read the eye-chart," she took me to Miriam's husband to get glasses for reading the board and for going to the movies.

However I think it was at Shula that I met Mary Wilner, that has always been my impression of where I met Mary. Altho it seems to me, my mother must have mentioned to Jane Pollock's mother, Gert— no! I bet I told Jane, my best friend who lived in the apartment above us, that I was being sent to Jewish Sunday school to learn Jewish history and how to read and write Yiddish, and Jane told her mother "Annie is going to Jewish School to learn Yiddish" and Gert must have asked Eleanor "where is the Jewish school? how much does it cost? I want Jane to learn Jewish history and how to write and read and speak Yiddish too."

And my mother was boxed in. She didn't want to tell Gert it is socialist Shula for the children of communists. So since the price was cheap enough, Gert decided Jane would go too, and my mother drove both me and Jane and picked me and Jane up when it was over. And fortunately Gert never found out it was socialist Shula for children of communists. They didn't teach any socialism or communism, it was strictly Jewish history, and how to read and write and speak Yiddish.

So Jane and I had sat together and had a great time when Miriam's son acted up, and Martin could not control him, and then Miriam was brought in and she couldn't control him either, that was really the high point of the morning.

Altho I always loved learning and loved to learn what I did there, it was just that it did not compare to playing, which is more fun. Yes I do think Mary showed up, so then it was Mary, me, and Jane. But the reason I became best friends with Mary is because my father was best friends with Mary's mother, Sadie, from "the Party."

This is why on the weekends, when we didn't drive over to visit our cousins, we would drive over to Mary's house instead, so Eleanor and Leon could visit Mary's mother and father, and I went to Mary's room and played with Mary. Or we went outside to play jump rope with Mary's friends.

To explain how much I loved Mary, you'd have to include how much I loved her house, her street, her neighborhood. I lived in an apartment in a housing project, a huge housing project, it stretched for miles in all directions. And right next to it was another housing project, huge, which stretched for miles. And all of this was built on a swamp in Flushing. I don't think there were any trees at all, just these new housing projects and new shopping centers.

There was nothing here for me, for my little girl's passion for beauty, and for mystery too. Altho I had a great childhood there, it was a flat dull world to look at. But where Mary lived was heaven for me. We rode for a long time till we came to some old part of Queens, it was all old houses, with slender, tree-shaded streets, curving roads, little roads, so many trees, all dark and shady and wonderful; and houses, houses are so much more interesting than identical apartments.

I loved Mary's neighborhood, I loved Mary's house, and what I loved most of all was going with Mary outside to the little little street with trees all around us, and playing jump-rope with her friends.

It is where I learned how to jump in backwards. We had a ball till night fell and I couldn't see the rope. And on Mary's 11th birthday party, Mary had a girls and boys party, and I had the ecstasy of playing Spin-the-Bottle and

Post Office which I loved.

It's possible the party even took place in the evening. Mary, for me, was a girl made out of treats.

All treats happened when I was with Mary, and especially at Mary's house, it was a world of treats which I didn't have in Electchester.

Of course we had great jump rope in Electchester too. We played it in one of the parking lots behind the building we lived in, and because of the projects, we had a lot more kids. There was a very long line when we played "Contest", which is the most fun game in the world, and I was always the leader for it. That was great jump-rope!

But there was nothing sweeter than jump-rope with Mary and her friends, in all that prettiness and sweetness of her neighborhood, it just made it such a treat.

I am sure mainly I went ice skating with Jane. First we would ice skate to our hearts content, we had our own ice skates. And then buy pizza and soft ice cream at the concession. Then when we finished ice skating, we would rent roller skates and play on the roller rink. But sometimes I went ice skating with Mary, she liked to ice skate too, and Mary was more special to me than Jane, because I didn't see her as often, Jane I took for granted, Mary was special.

Maybe my mother was nice enough to drive all the way to Mary's house to pick up Mary, or maybe Mary's father brought her. I just remember waiting on the line to get in with Mary with our ice skates around our neck. In the dream all that came out about Mary was going ice skating with her, that we both put red pompoms on our ice skates together, and that she came to my 8th birthday party. Maybe I learned about pompoms from Mary and then Jane and I made them for our ice skates. It is logical I would learn them from Mary because all treats derived from Mary.

The game I played with Mary when we were in her house was "Sense and Nonsense" which was based on a tv show then. But we would skip all the other senses, touch smell sight etc and go right to "taste" which meant we went to Mary's kitchen and ate all the delicious food which she always had in her kitchen.

And one Christmas her parents invited our family over for Christmas dinner. My parents rebelled against the Jewish religion too but they don't go so far as to have Christmas dinner. It was the only Christmas dinner I ever had as a child.

Then Mary's parents bought a ranch style house in Long

Island, near Jones Beach, we visited once or twice but it ended the friendship, because I never saw Mary after that.

And maybe never even thought about her after that, till I began going to the Paradox in the East Village, a macrobiotic restaurant, and there was a guy there who sold belts on a rack, I remember that because when I began to date Bill he bought one of the belts. His name was Jonathan. Jonathan and I became friends, he was quite attractive, and he told me he was dating Mary Wilner.

"Mary Wilner!" I said.

"Mary Wilner" he said.

"I know Mary Wilner" I said, "where does she live?"

"On 11th Street."

"On 11th Street!" I said, "take me to her!"

And he took me over to an East Village tenement apartment on 11th Street and there was Mary all grown up now, a young woman with very long hair, she always had long hair, even in that photo of her at my birthday party she had her long hair.

And I said "Jonathan is cute," and she said she doesn't really go for him, so I said "can I go out with him," and she said "fine." But I think I just had one date with Jonathan, if it was even a date. Because Bill became my boyfriend instead, and has been ever since.

I saw Mary about 10 times after that. She and I were both school teachers, her school was near Columbia. I remember telling her as we were walking along First Avenue together "I have decided to give up shoplifting" and Mary said she shoplifts all the time, and the problem is she shoplifts in the same stores where the kids in her class shoplift.

I guess Mary and I didn't really stay friends, we drifted apart. There wasn't anything to hold us together now, nothing was happening between us. It was kind of like the shell of a seed, the left-over shell; once the seed has sprouted and turned into a beautiful flower, the beautiful flower was our friendship back then, and finding each other now was just the left-over shell, we had outgrown our friendship.

Altho there was a taken-for-granted warmth and intimacy, it was accepted between us we loved each other, but we didn't click in any way, it seemed a little empty.

Then Bill moved in with me, we began our life together. I quit school teaching and began working part time in various places, first at the Museum for Lew Irizarri again, then at the Museum Shop downstairs, and then for a Wall Street newspaper.

And maybe it was towards the late '70s that someone who knew Mary and me (but who would? maybe Amy Kalish) said "Mary is living in California now and she is the girlfriend of the guy who started Esalon."

It was some famous name from the '60s and I was surprised Mary was with a guy who was our parents' age, also that some famous guy in CA our parents' age chose Mary for his girlfriend. I couldn't understand it. I just thought Mary and I sure went different ways, here I am with Bill in my East Village apartment, and she is out in California with a much older man, whose name everyone knows because he started Esalon or something like that, something very California ....

And I guess you could say that was my last contact with Mary, till she showed up so beautiful and happy and glowing in my dream last night.

Love, Anne

How I moved to Tucson

Warm May-like pretty Spring day. Slight breeze ruffling the leaves. O I can feel it on my face too. It is very gentle. That is the call of the cactus wren. It is spirited. 3 birds took off together, they all alit on my mesquite tree. They twittered for an instant and took off. One alit for an instant on my windowsill on its way to somewhere. It was a sparrow. It sure changes my view that now I look thru a bank of green leaves. I like this kelly green world. It is a happy day. I can feel the wellspring of happiness.

O sparrow is on the branch. Their tummies are dovegrey. The sky has some white streaky clouds to the north. And I can see some fainter ones to the west. And if I look straight up I can see some there too. I can see thru the small mesquite tree right out my window to the huge mesquite tree in middle of my yard.

O there is Bill arriving in yard, with his cup o' coffee. He is wearing checked pajama bottoms, white tee shirt, carrying cup o' coffee in one hand and *How to fix bicycles* manual in other hand, and his Jets hat.

He is in the middle of the greenery, all I can see is his arm. O I see his system. He puts down the big cup of coffee on the ground, picks it up for sip or two, puts it back on the ground and opens up his how to fix bicycles book. Hahaha he is camouflaged by the leaves.

Jim in pool told me all the beautiful places he had visited. The islands in the Caribbean where he snorkeled and windsailed with his wife Annie. The islands of Maui and another beautiful island in Hawaii. He tried to describe the beauty of the waterfalls on Maui by referring to *Indiana Jones*. "Remember the part in the beginning in the jungle, that was filmed there." I really didn't remember it at all but I said I did.

Maybe he read my mind because he said "remember Bali Hai in *South Pacific*, it was filmed there." This time he connected. How can I ever forget the scenes from Bali Hai. They are etched into my brain. I saw the movie at the Valencia in Jamaica, Queens when I was a teenager. It must have been on a weekend afternoon, and I took the bus, and went by myself. Movies in the movie theater are framed by the experience of going to them. Where I was then in life, and where the movie theater was located. *South Pacific* is framed by Jamaica Queens and seen thru the eyes of 16 year old young woman who drank it all in.

It is funny to be in a swimming pool in Tucson Arizona, halfway to Bali Hai, recollecting it now with Jim. It gave me the feeling I had reached half way to the paradise I had drank in in the Valencia movie theater in Jamaica. The problem I had with Jim's conversation about all the wondrous beauties he had experienced, is I kept feeling paradise was somewhere out there far away, in the distance, and where I was, was not paradise.

And the truth is I left NYC to live in Tucson because I wanted to live in paradise. To Jim paradise is enchanted waterfalls in all that lushness, and swimming underwater and looking at unbelievable color, green and red coral reefs, with gorgeous fish swimming around it. Jim who was born on the desert is starved for water, beauty, color, lushness. But I love the peace the desert brings. Would I want to give up our flawless blue sky, which is always blue?

It wasn't a random choice to move to the southwestern desert. It began off in my dreams when I still lived in NYC.

There were a series of dreams for a month or two. And when the dreams ended I had arrived in Tucson. Altho naturally I had no idea that is where my dreams were leading me. I did not expect to move. I still remember the first dream:

In that dream I visited the palace of great glowing Goddess. The palace is where the Goddess dwelt. I didn't know whether it was in California, Arizona, or Nevada. I was vague about the Southwest when I lived in NYC. But it was somewhere in the Southwest.

At the time I didn't know the dream had anything to do with me, I woke up in the morning just lost in the glory of having spent the night with a Goddess in a palace in the glowing Southwest. I just felt so privileged and so blessed to have had that dream. I felt touched by the divine.

But it was at the point when I was still writing down my dreams in a book each morning, and I remember now the dreams continued, nothing like the Goddess and being at her palace, but all having to do with being in California. I think in my dreams it was always California, but the CA of the Southwest.

These dreams continued as my NYC life collapsed around me, and finally the definitive dreams began.

I dreamt I was at the candy store, Gem Spa. Originally an old NYC cigar store, which sold magazines, ice cream cones, and fountain drinks, on the corner of St Mark's Place and 2nd Avenue, a few blocks from my apartment. And I ordered a chocolate egg cream. In my dream I said to myself "this is my last chocolate egg cream from Gem Spa." Then I crossed 2nd Avenue to head home, and 2nd Avenue changed from a city block on the Lower East Side, to desert, heading steeply down to water down below, and I started to head into the desert.

That could have been an afternoon dream when I dozed off, or was the dream the night before, because the following night

I dreamt my big cousin John was in NYC from San Francisco, and he saw a beautiful Monet painting he wanted, it must have been "Water Lilies." He did not know if he should buy it, but I consulted with his mom, my aunt Esther, who was in Heaven, but in my dream she was available to consult. "Go for it!" she said. So I said to John "go for it!" I told John "I am a great Girl Friday, I will bubble wrap your painting to death, insure it for a million dollars, and send it to you." So John decided to buy it.

That evening as I sat at my kitchen table with my life in smithereens again and I asked my Higher Self the old familiar question, "what should I do?" I didn't get the old familiar answer. The old familiar answer was always:

"Do nothing, I love you, calm down, have a cigarette, have a cup of coffee, have a piece of cake, have a second piece of cake, here let me pour a cup of coffee for you and cut you a piece of cake."

This time the answer I got was *"Move."*

"Move where?" I asked.

"Move to Tucson, your aunt is there, she can help you."

"But what about all my stuff?"

"Just leave it behind" she said, "take your writing and your computer and that's all."

"But how can we get there, we have a dog and no drivers license and no car?"

"Take the airplane, the airplane accepts dogs."

"But how can I do it, if I can't even think about it?"

"Don't think about it," she said, "just do it."

So now I knew the decision was up to me. I was terrified to decide yes. But I did. And instantly I made the decision I knew it was the right decision. I was flooded with liberation. I knew I had decided to be free and I was free. In that instant I had left NYC. I hadn't arrived in the Southwest yet, but an old life ended, new one had begun.

Deciding to move to Tucson was an earthquake for me

My Higher Self has me buy new truck

Celia is the youngest of my father's siblings. She is 12 years younger than my father, and 13 years younger than Esther, the eldest. Franny is Celia's Tucson friend, a few years younger than she. Franny was also my first friend when I moved to Tucson. Because she found the apt. for her friend Celia's niece, me. And lived in the same apt. complex, and befriended me when we first arrived.

When I first decided to move to Tucson, I called my cousin Pete and asked him to find me an apt. which accepted dogs. My aunt Celia was in Tucson, her son Pete was in Tucson, and the youngest of her 4 children, Bobby. Her other two children were living in California.

I chose Pete, because when my dad was driving my aunt Esther and me back to Manhattan after a family gathering at his house, my dad and his sister gossiped in the front seat. All their concern was about their baby sister in Tucson. When she no longer had a husband, they took over worrying about her and being in charge of her. It was the '60s, and they were very concerned about Celia's report that her son Pete was now living with the Jesus Freaks.

My dad said "but they have a good record of getting kids off drugs."

And my aunt Esther said "but we don't know Pete is on drugs."

I was so young myself then that I had no judgment about my cousin Pete in Tucson living with the Jesus Freaks. I merely thought it was interesting. But by the time I decided to leave NYC and move to Tucson, Jesus was a big part of my life. And it made me feel close to my cousin Pete in Tucson that he believed in Jesus, which is why I chose him to call and ask for help.

I confided that to Pete after I had been in Tucson for several months, I told him why I chose him to call and ask for help. There was a long silence and finally he said, "that was an embarrassing episode in my life and I don't believe in Jesus." So much for having so much in common. But I guess it served its purpose. I needed to feel close to someone to ask for help.

It had made me feel close to Pete. And Pete had delivered help. He had found me an apt in apt complex called Willow Brook which accepted dogs, and which was the price I wanted to pay, $300 a month. But it fell thru because dog could not weigh over 33 pounds and Clio weighed 37 pounds. But I was immensely encouraged. Then I got phone call from Celia saying Pete had tried and not succeeded so he had turned the job over to her, and she had consulted apartment finders. "It is not easy to find apt in Tucson which accepts dogs."

Then I got the phone call the apt had been found. I had asked for one bedroom for $300. I was sure I could not afford bigger apt. But Celia had found 2 bedroom for $330. "Great! take it!" I said. "Drive right over! put down the money and take it! I will send you money order for it." And that is the apartment we moved into two weeks later.

It turned out Celia had been visiting her friend Franny and said to Franny "what I really want for my niece is an apartment like yours, Franny."

So Franny said "let's go over to management and see if they have any."

And sure enough they had the two bedroom for $330.

And when Celia called me, I said "grab it, drive over now and put the money down." And Celia drove over and put the money down. And when she got back home she said "the apartment is yours."

And I said "great!"

We had already started packing up all our stuff in boxes, but we now had an address to send them to.

And when we walked into our new Tucson apartment in the middle of the night two weeks later there was a note from Franny with a jar of salsa as a gift. The note gave helpful hints and welcomed us. Unfortunately Franny had forgotten how old-fashioned NYC is. We shivered at night in the Tucson apt. for a whole month before Franny showed us how to turn on the heat.

Back in NYC at around 5 o'clock on cold winter nights, you would hear the reassuring gurgle of the steam in the radiator. It meant the landlord had turned on the furnace. And at 5 pm in Tucson, when Sun went down and it turned ice cold, I listened for that reassuring gurgle but it never came. I had no idea there was a dial, which you could set at any temperature you want, and be as toasty warm as you wanted to be, and didn't have to wait for the landlord to decide to give you heat.

Franny had walked with me a few mornings when I walked my dog. She was the only person I knew in Tucson, I was grateful to have her as a friend. Franny told me all about herself, and I did learn a lot about Franny's life as a result, altho I could not absorb any of it at the time.

She did say one very practical thing tho. She pointed to the mountains which were always in view, and said "that is north." After that I stopped worrying I would get lost when I took my dog out in the morning, I knew I could always orient myself from the mountains.

The new truck

When we first moved to Tucson my cousin Pete had just bought himself a new compact truck. It was his first new car, all the others had been second hand. He liked having a new car so much that when we planned to buy a secondhand car and Pete was taking us around to lots, he found a brand new Isuzu compact truck on sale at the dealership for $5200 and suggested we buy it, which we did.

I don't even think Bill was at home when Pete arrived with truck from the dealership. I got in the truck with him. We went back to dealership together, Pete took the truck for test drive with me in it, I consulted with my Higher Self, and I bought it.

My aunt had told my father "Annie has to have good used car, send her 3 or 4 thousand," so my dad had sent $5000 for good used car. And the truck Pete had found was $5200 so I had the money in the bank for it. So I just asked my Higher Self, and she said "go for it."

And Pete and I did the paper work with the dealership man, Greg. We became friends. And then Pete drove the truck home for me, since I don't know how to drive.

By now Bill was back home. I didn't know how to break the news to him. I wasn't sure he would like it. He had his own ideas of what he wanted in a vehicle and this was not his idea. Plus he only knew how to drive automatic, he had just finished his driving lessons and passed his test, he was new driver.

So Pete was very surprised when the conversation was so desultory. Bill was talking about the Wildcats and I was going along with the flow of that conversation, how the team was doing, and then maybe the conversation had segued into food. And finally Pete looked at me aghast. "Aren't you going to tell him!"

And I said "O yeah right. Bill, I just bought a brand new

truck."

Bill was stunned and Pete got on the phone to tell his girlfriend. He was thrilled at the deal he had worked out for me. He told his girlfriend all about it in the happy exited joyous way he had thought I would tell Bill.

We just sat there quietly while Pete told his girlfriend all about our new truck. That is how Bill found out all about it. Then Pete said "you will need insurance," so he called his insurance, Farmer's, but they wouldn't give it to Bill, he is new driver. So he called Greg at dealership and Greg told him where we can go to get insurance if we are new driver.

And then Pete left to go home and Bill said "I don't want it."

He said "I am a brand new driver, I don't want a brand new shiny red truck, I will feel self conscious, I want what I planned, beat up old car, while I am still getting the feel for driving, and I don't know how to do a stick shift."

So next day Greg from the dealership came over to teach Bill how to do the stick. And the day after that he had his driving teacher come over for another lesson and they did stick shift together, and after that Bill knew how to do the stick shift. But he still didn't want the fancy new red truck.

"Take it back!" he said.

"I won't" I said.

But it worked out. He started his yard working business and a pick-up truck was very convenient for that. He loaded all his tools on it and yard working means when you finish the job you take all the weeds and branches you have trimmed to the dump. And he felt much more comfortable once it had turned into a work truck.

In retrospect I understand. I understand Bill's feelings and why he didn't want it. But I also see why his idea, we buy small old beat up sedan, was not a good idea. When we first got truck we didn't know a month or two down the line, Bill would decide to open up yard working business and the truck was perfect for that. And having all this experience now of car trouble and huge car repair bills with the 2nd hand Chrysler 5th Avenue we bought 7 years later, it was smart to buy brand new truck which never had any car trouble at all.

That is the whole deal when you make a decision based on what your Higher Self tells you instead of going by your feelings. Your feelings only describe what makes you feel comfortable in the moment. But with our Higher Self a decision is made which takes in a much bigger picture. 12 years later I can see all the reasons why it was exactly the right vehicle for us. For 13 years it has served all our needs perfectly. Bill took perfect care of it and it still runs perfectly. And when we bought the house a year later we needed it to move our stuff plus all the things we bought for the house.

It caused a lot of commotion in our relationship that I tuned into my Higher Self 7 years before Bill did. Because I made all decisions based on Her suggestions and the suggestions were never what we felt comfortable with at the time, but were always ways to renovate our life, to expand opportunity.

I had already formed the habit of going along with her suggestions, instead of my own feelings, for everything in my own life. I had discovered her suggestions all worked. I trusted her and them.

But when it came to our life together, and I carried out her suggestions, I bought the new truck and I bought the house, Bill was extremely upset that I had gone ahead and done things which were the opposite of his feelings. He could not understand why I was acting how I was. And that I was unbudgeable about it. I couldn't explain about my Higher Self, he wouldn't have understood.

Shopping at Fry's and Cousin Pete buys New Truck

Sunday morning. Early. Sun has just risen over mountain. Desert is wet and dripping from big rain last night. Earth is moist and spongy. A sparrow hip hops on it. It is all woodsy fragrant now. But once our huge desert Sun has gained altitude and shines on my backyard the woodsy world will evaporate.

The rain was so big that when Bill and I returned home from supermarket yesterday evening we rode thru flooded streets. Bill was scared our truck would stall in the deep water and we were driving on major thoroughfare.

I let the woman on line at supermarket go ahead of me because she was just buying a small bottle of soda and I had a whole week's shopping there. I had watched her go over to the case and select which beverage she wanted, and then she stood behind me. "Go ahead" I said, "you only have that and I have all this."

She gestured her thanks. And then to my surprise I saw her entering her pin number.

"Sorry" the checkout girl said, "it didn't work, do it again."

After the machine would not accept 4 entries by her, checkout girl said "you are only allowed 4 tries."

So woman took out a huge wallet filled with credit cards, extracted a 20 dollar bill and received change. Then she gestured her thanks to all of us and left.

I had assumed she was a very poor woman, and when her card didn't work I thought I would pay for her soda rather than her have to leave it behind. I still can't figure out why she would try to pay for the soda with her pin number when she had twenty in her wallet. I said to the checkout girl "why did she use her card when she had a twenty, would you ever do that?"

The checkout girl said "no."

I said "no one does that."

The checkout girl said "you'd be surprised." And then I realized she had seen every kind of peculiar behavior.

"I guess you've seen everything" I said.

"Yes" she said.

One of the items I had bought was Stouffer's frozen lasagna. It had been on sale for half price. She picked it up and looked at it for a long time.

"Is it good?" she asked me.

I didn't know how to answer. I said "well I used to live in Little Italy when I lived back in New York City, I know what good Italian food tastes like."

As soon as I said "Little Italy" the young guy bagging my groceries looked up. "I love Italian food" he said, "it is the best."

"Me too, Italian and Mexican."

The checkout girl said that is her favorite too.

But he said "I am Mexican and I think Italian food is the best."

I looked out and saw that it was pouring.

"Did you know it was raining?"

"Yes" she said, and made a face.

I was so surprised. In all my time in Tucson everyone unanimously and universally has greeted the advent of rain with jubilation. In fact this is the first time ever since I have been on the desert that I have been in a store and looked out the windows at checkout counter and saw rain coming down.

Rain is just not casual, frequent, random, on the desert. It only occurs during certain times of year and then only during certain times of day. We are in monsoon season now and the rain arrives around 5 pm, and this is about the time I looked out the supermarket glass doors. But it was still strange. I have never once walked out of the store into a parking lot with rain coming down.

And then we drove home thru flooded streets, it must have been raining the whole time I was in the supermarket.

Each time we passed a white truck I asked Bill "is that what Pete's brand new truck looks like?" Last week at swimming pool he told us he bought a brand new white full sized Ford truck that day.

"I bought myself the truck of my dreams," he said, "but I am too self conscious to drive it. Does Bill want to buy it?"

"It is the truck of Bill's dreams, but we don't have the money for it now."

"Ask your Higher Self how I can sell it," he asked.

"OK I will."

"I just want an old beat up truck that I don't have to think twice about getting into.

Emissions Test

Well it is Spring today. I knew when I woke up winter was over, spring had started, and the beginning of the long season culminating in summer had begun.

I knew it when I woke up because the idea of summer, which had been intangible all winter, suddenly became tangible to me, I knew it was on the agenda. Not that I am in a rush for a long hotter-than-hell desert summer but I love the long preamble of spring leading up to it. And I love it that the world of cold and dark, which winter brings, is over. Basically what we have now is delightful, and it will stay delightful till there is too much delight for us to bear, too much light and too much heat.

Yesterday we brought our 2nd hand Chrysler Fifth Avenue in for emissions test. I got out of the car and went into the little house when the girl began to do the emissions test with Bill. I went in to write out the check for the new tag. The woman who works there remembered me and we had a ball yukking it up about stuff.

She said "I don't remember this car, I thought you have the other car."

I said "we have the truck but this car was bought for me to learn how to drive on."

"Did you learn?" she said.

"Not yet" I said.

"My mom is not happy" I said "because she sent me the money for the driving lessons, but the money she sent was exactly enough to buy this car so I bought it, and now she is mad that I didn't use the money for what it is for, she really wants me to drive and so does my husband."

The e-test woman said "Anne it is time for you to learn how to drive, and next time I want to see you bringing in the car for emissions test."

I got so happy. She had so much confidence in me. We were chatting and giggling so much I said to her "did you tell my husband he passed emissions, he worries so much."

She said "yes I told him to pull the car over." She said "men worry too much that is their whole problem."

When I got back in the car Bill said "did it pass?"

I said "yes, didn't the girl tell you, she said she did."

"All she said was pull the car over."

"She wants me to bring the car in for emissions next year."

"This is good car for you to drive on, Anne, because it wouldn't matter if it got scraped or bumped, your idea that you will win the lottery and buy yourself a brand new Buick to drive isn't such a good idea because you wouldn't want to scrape up your brand new car."

Then we went to Lane Bryant so I could show them the zipper on the skirt I bought last summer won't go down and I am afraid to keep pulling at it because I don't want to break the zipper.

The manager said "all I can do is give you 7 dollars which is what the skirt was on clearance."

I said "but I paid more than that for it."

But she said "unless you have your tags or receipt it is all I can do."

Actually it was generous offer because I wore the skirt a handful of times. But eventually she got the zipper to work.

I said "should I take home the skirt, or accept the 7 dollars?"

She said "take home your skirt and if the zipper doesn't

work again bring it back and I will give you the 7 dollars."

The pink skirt is very pretty but I had discovered it doesn't really go with anything, plus it looks like it could pick up stain so easily, but I decided to take it home and keep my options open.

I said "do you have anything pretty on clearance while I am here?" And she showed me long sleeved soft V-necked tops in every conceivable color.

"Which is your favorite color?" I asked.

And she took out the red one so I bought it.

Then I said to Bill "take me to Park Mall so I can go to Victoria's Secret and buy that lovely perfume."

The girl at swimming pool last year had sprayed perfume on herself and when I said "what is that lovely scent?" she said "*Amber Romance* from Victoria's Secret" and she let me spray it on myself.

Then yesterday morning when I was walking Lulu, Lulu went up to the teenage girl on her way to high school. "That perfume you are wearing is lovely, what is it?" I asked. I couldn't understand her Spanish accent so she took it out of her purse to show me. It was *Amber Romance* from Victoria's Secret. I thought since I liked it two times I will buy it.

Park Mall is no longer the sleepy little mall it used to be when it was my favorite mall. It is now tremendously fancy. They put in 6-plex movie theater, they brought a lot of fancy stores to it, they have a food court and fancy restaurants, the whole works, and it is now impossible to find a parking place.

Finally Bill let me off and said "you can find me in the car, if I'm not there I went to the bookstore, wait for me."

I bought *Amber Romance*. It was $9 for one bottle, but for $35 I could have 8. I could have given one to Jan, and to Mary, Bill's sis, and Bonnie my brother's wife, and to Bill's mom, to Margot, and to my friends at swim pool.

It was hard choice, but I am on a budget, and just bought one. Then I looked for the car and could not find it. I went back to the court and said to the security guard "I can't find my car or my husband" and just then Bill got up. He had been waiting there for me.

So then we went to Discount Foods to get Lulu her Kraft's singles. Discount Foods is the exact opposite experience of being in Victoria's Secret in a very very fancy mall. People shop at Discount Foods because they don't want to pay supermarket prices and supermarket prices are so low anyway. But my little Lulu likes 6 slices of individually wrapped Kraft's singles each morning when she wakes up. I can buy family pack (72 slices) at Fry's for $8, but one day I was in Discount Foods and noticed they had 5 times that amount for almost the same price. The bargain is irresistible to me.

However at Discount Foods you can never count on them having what you want. I asked the man if he had it and he was so apologetic about not having it. Altho he had cheddar cheese singles and I thought maybe Lulu would like that.

I said "I bought a meatloaf here last time and my husband liked it, do you know where it is?"

And he walked right over and showed it to me.

"You know how happy it makes you when your husband likes the food you buy" I said to him, and he understood perfectly.

He was such a nice man and so understanding. And then I got a loaf of sliced white bread because we were out of that.

When I got to check-out counter the man was asking the Spanish lady how she was going to get home. I thought she said "I will take the bus and then walk a mile," so I instantly said "where do you live?"

She said "Country Club Road."

I said "we are going to Country Club Road, let my husband drive you."

I had a hard time understanding her accent. So the check-out man helped me. We figured out she lives on Speedway, between Country Club and Dodge, near the Pontiac dealer. The check-out man was overjoyed, he did not want her to have to take the bus, "she will save money too this way," he said to me. He said "today is Saint Patrick's Day, I knew it would be a good day."

She waited till I paid for my groceries and we walked to car together. Bill was happy to drive her.

He said to me "your stuff is all over the front seat, your bag from Victoria's Secret."

I said "let her sit in front seat, that is more fun, I can put all my stuff in the back, plus her groceries."

The check-out man had said "just let her off at Speedway and Dodge, she can cross the street by herself." But Bill was able to do a U-turn when we reached Dodge Road and there was the huge Pontiac dealer, and we drove in the little street and there was her apartment complex.

In the car I told Bill "I bought cheese for Lulu, meatloaf, and bread and that's all."

"I'm glad you bought the meatloaf" he said, "it goes good with mashed potatoes."

"But I don't have mashed potatoes" I said.

"We can have boiled potatoes" he said, "that is perfect for St Patrick's Day."

When we reached the woman's house (I hadn't realized she heard our conversation), she said she has potatoes in the house, can she give us some.

I said "O that is so nice of you but I have some potatoes at home."

She wanted to give me a dollar, she had it in her hand, "please" she said, "please."

But it had given Bill and me such joy to do the favor for her, and she might like having her extra dollar so I didn't accept it, but gave her a kiss.

Alice

I was swimming in my lane yesterday, pool was practically empty on such chilly morning, when Alice arrived, just the girl I wanted to see. "Alice" I said "I want to ask your advice about something."

My friend Maggie from internet sent me email asking me to buy her a silver and malachite pendant to go on a necklace, she will reimburse me. So when I saw Alice yesterday I said "my friend Maggie wants a pendant which is malachite and silver."

Alice said "the gem show is in town, I will look for malachite and silver pendant for your friend." She said the girl who made my necklace has been her friend for 30 years, she is an Indian and married to our State Senator.

Alice said she used to make jewelry and she likes her own jewelry even better than her friend's. And then without missing a beat, somehow what went on was the story of Alice's whole life. No writer on earth could reproduce what Alice told me as we swam back and forth in the lanes. And she did not tell it in an orderly way. Apparently there were two main chapters but she kept saying one detail from one chapter and another detail from another chapter.

The first chapter, she was married to sound engineer in New York City. The sound studio was behind Lincoln Center. It was assumed Harry Belafonte owned it but apparently it was really owned by Tammy who Alice has never met. And Alice is outraged now that she heard Tammy is living as bag woman in Central Park. She thinks the sound studio was stolen from Tammy. All the stories of the sound studio era involve millions, mayhem, and even violence. Cars going after cars when they went to Jamaica, and her neck got broken. Her husband sounds terrible but they had a beautiful son together. Alice said she worked on 4 songs which were on the Hit Parade.

The next chapter is 25 years living in the Yucatan where she was kidnapped by a big Indian Chief and became his wife. Altho he was such a big Indian Chief, Alice was not his only wife, which was what upset her. They had beautiful son together too. Living with the Indians in the Yucatan is where Alice learned to speak Indian, to weave, and to make her own jewelry.

She said she likes to be creative. "Most people want stones which are dull color and match, who wants that! it looks like string of pearls, I like vivid colors and odd shapes for stones."

As far as I can make out there was violence in the Yucatan too. She got robbed there. She said "in Mexico if you yell out 'help' no one will come, but if you yell out 'vagina' everyone will come."

That tickled my funny bone. "Thanks for the useful info Alice, I will remember that when I get to Mexico, yell out vagina when I want help."

But she didn't get my joke. She said how she had met an Indian there and he said "your vagina needs help, let me examine it." That is what led her to explain how yelling out vagina is the way to get help in Mexico. She got concerned when I said "now I know what to do when I get to Mexico." She said "you don't know how handsome those Indians are, it is unbelievable, but they are Romeos, they will break your heart, you will be taken in by them." I wasn't worried about being taken in by handsome Indian Romeos, I have my Higher Self plus I am happy with Bill.

After long tales of mayhem and violence things began to settle down when she began to talk about raising her two sons. It sounds like she had a happy home with them even tho neither husband helped out. The son of the Yucatan Indian Chief lives in Tucson and is straight as anyone can be, wears designer clothes, drives a designer sports car, is taking Business Administration at the U of A, is married and has two kids. The son of the sound engineer lives in NYC and is a computer nerd, and won't go to college.

"His girlfriend is Puerto Rican but she won't pick up her clothes or cook meals or clean the house."

"She sounds like me" I said to Alice, and Alice was shocked I am like that.

She can't figure out why the son of the Indian Chief is such a neat freak. "I never raised my sons like that, we had happy relaxed home, he has one of those empty houses where everything is put away out of sight."

She said because she raised both sons without a father in the home they each think they are her father. When she told her New York son yesterday she put in the concrete to make a driveway, she got scolded. "Concrete attracts damp, Mother, and beside you're not supposed to be working with concrete."

"What damp!" she said to me, "we live on the desert, it is dry as a bone here."

By now we were moving into normal life. Alice confided she watches television now. "I never watched television before" she said, "I don't know what is happening to me."

"I like science fiction" she said.

"I like *Matlock* and *Murder She Wrote*" I said.

And then Alice talked about the TV shows she watches. Alice confided she is looking for a boyfriend but wonders if she has a chance at 62.

I said "Alice, my friend Ruthie who lives in San Diego who has a solution to everything told me this." And to my shock, Alice, who had been lost for a solid hour in mayhem and violence and vagina and being kidnapped by big Indian chiefs in the Yucatan jungle, moved very close to me to hear every word about what my friend Ruthie said about finding a boyfriend when you are 62.

I told Alice I had told my friend Ruthie I was extremely upset to notice that the woman Bush chose for the Supreme Court had lost all her prettiness and she is not old. And Ruthie said, "Anne last night *Hillside Blues* was on, it was a rerun. The young man was arrested for stealing his aunt's money. The young man said 'why am I arrested, my 62 year old aunt has men in the house all the time, she put up a personal ad saying, if you want great sex call me up, the result is there are men in the house all the time, go ask them if they took her money.' So the handsome young detective went to interview the aunt, then he had an affair with her, and then he married her."

Alice was immensely relieved and happy to hear that. She said "I do go out with young men all the time but they grab my ass and my breasts and I don't like that."

I said "there is no reason why they can't behave like gentlemen, wait till you find the right guy."

"But I don't like to go to bars" she said.

"You never find anyone in a bar" I said.

"I come here to the club and I haven't met anyone here I like."

"Just be patient" I said.

She said "my parents died young and I was adopted." She said "I have no experience in picking the right man, all the men I pick are lemons."

I said "where did you grow up Alice?"

She said "New York."

I said "I am from New York too, which part?"

She said "our sound stage was right behind Lincoln Center."

I said "which part of New York did you grow up in, which high school did you go to?"

She said "I was born in Syracuse."

I said "my mom came from Rochester."

She said "my grandfather had a department store there but it went out of business." She said "my dad was Mayor."

"Mayor of what?" I asked.

"Mayor of Syracuse and Rochester" and she named another town.

I said to Bill in the car "does Alice exaggerate?"

"Why?" he said.

"She said her dad was mayor of Syracuse and two other towns, you can't be mayor of 3 towns all at once."

"Maybe it wasn't all at once" he said.

"She said she did a 1000 hours of work for free for a man on his film at Tucson Access Studio and when she asked him to get her a container of coffee he said 'I don't owe you anything bitch,' and she was so upset she went outside to have a cigarette.

"She said 'don't tell Bill I had a cigarette, he disapproves of smoking.'

"I said 'my Bill?' she said 'yes.'

"I said 'but I smoke a lot of cigarettes, when Bill wants a cigarette he comes to me, he only smokes 3 or 4, but I am internet addict and smoke all the time on the computer.'

"She said 'I didn't know you smoked cigarettes Anne, ok I will admit to you I went outside and had a cigarette.'"

I said to Bill "I didn't know you were one of those people who tell people to give up cigs when they admit they smoke cigs."

Bill went apoplectic in the car.

"I never once mentioned cigarettes to Alice in the steam room. Where did she get that idea? Maybe she meant the other Bill, but the other Bill smokes cigars all the time and besides he isn't like that. There is another Bill from New York City, he doesn't like smoke, maybe Alice means him."

Bill was so upset at hearing Alice said he disapproved of smoking and tries to make people stop, that he lost interest in whether Alice's dad really was Mayor of 3 cities. He kept returning to the smoking topic, trying to figure out where Alice got the idea. I was going to tell him Alice said if I ever need help in Mexico just yell out vagina, but Bill is Catholic, Catholics never find sex funny.

Afternoon at Alice's House

Alice got offered to do a series of shows on Access TV Tucson. First she planned to do it on bands, she had worked in the music business back in NYC, and she began asking the guys at our club if they had a band. Then she decided to switch it to women. So I told her I write short stories, but I don't want to be on tv, I want someone else to read them. And Alice said fine.

When Lily was swimming in next lane from me I asked Lily if she would be willing to read my stories on Alice's tv show. Lily said she loves to read out loud and she would be happy to do it, so I was overjoyed.

Lily works full time and the date which Alice had rented the studio at Access, Saturday, was the day Lily was helping her friend with huge yard sale. So we decided we would all go to Alice's house on the previous Saturday, which was last Saturday, and Alice said she would ask her friend Roy to work the camera.

Roy has his own show with Access, "The Roy Show," but they take turns working the camera for each other. So Alice gave me and Lily instructions on how to get to her house.

Tucson is an odd town. Because you drive practically to Tucson Mall, which is the busiest part of all of Tucson, but before you get there, you make a right, and then another right, and then follow a dirt road till the end, and there is Alice's house.

And it is like a little house in the country. Completely quiet there, with doves and quail in her backyard. And a hawk who hangs around, and marches himself into Alice's house and preens his feathers for her.

Alice's house is not like a suburban house, it is like a little house someone built themselves a long long time ago. And it is in an old part of Tucson, it was there way before the Tucson Mall was there, and way before Tucson had turned into thriving metropolis. It is also near Oracle Road because Oracle used to be the main drag back then, it still is, which is why it is the busiest part of Tucson.

I didn't see all of Alice's house. I saw the little living room and the little kitchen. And next door to it, she had built a studio. When we arrived (Bill drove) we went into the living room, where Alice's paintings in frames were wall-to-wall up on living room.

They are glorious paintings with beautiful color. Obviously she had framed them all because she wanted them in a gallery. And you can just imagine how, in a huge white gallery with enough space to set off each painting, it would be thrilling sight.

Bill came in for just a few minutes and was excited to see her paintings. He did not stay. Two basketball championship games were on back-to-back that afternoon, and he was going to watch them at our swim club.

Roy was sitting and smoking a cigarette on chair by the couch. He looked like very nice man. So I lit a cigarette and sat down next to him. Lily rushed out of the room then because she said she is one of those people who doesn't like smoke.

Roy said "tell me about the story Lily is going to read."

And I said "it is an experience of mine."

When I said that, his eyes glazed over. But there was no way to describe the story, and beside he was going to hear it when Lily read it.

So Roy played two shows for us he did (two episodes of

"The Roy Show") so we could see what access shows look like. In the first one a woman dressed up in clothes she thought Emily Dickinson would wear and enacted a poem by Emily Dickinson. She didn't read it from a page, she stood up and dramatized it. I found it very interesting.

I know nothing at all about Emily Dickinson and was surprised to discover she was a bitch. Maybe that is too strong a word. As far as I could make out Emily was saying how much she enjoys freaking out the neighbors. I applauded when it was over, it was dramatic and held my interest.

The next show was Roy reading article from Tucson newspaper about a murder. Apparently a doctor who had 17 girlfriends was stabbed 13 times. The Medical Examiner could not determine when it was done within a 24 hour period. But the Prosecuting Attorney, who had someone on trial, insisted it was done during the one hour period he had the person on trial for. It appeared to have happened in a restaurant. It was quite confusing. It was Roy and Alice sitting at a table discussing it. And Alice pointed out "how did he know it took place during that one hour period."

I applauded when that show was over because it was so much fun watching Alice poke all those holes in the DA's case.

Then we went into Alice's studio where Lily was going to read my story. It began with Lily and Alice sitting together and talking, but each time it started Roy stopped the camera and said "move an inch to the right." So each time they built up a head of steam, it was stopped. Finally Roy decided he got it right, but by then they just said two sentences to each other, and Alice stepped out of the frame and Lily read the story.

She did an OK job. It is hard when someone doesn't know the story. As a writer you put in a lot of teeny details just to flesh it out. They are actually irrelevant but are what bring a story to life. Lily gave a lot of emphasis to all these teeny details, and they were meaningless. And some parts which had meaning, she didn't get, so the meaning didn't come across. But it was OK job. I felt if I wasn't willing to do it myself, and Lily was willing to do it, that I was grateful Lily did it. And there were moments when the story did go along fine.

"Good job, Lily" I said, and I meant it. I thought she did fine job.

Both Alice and Roy were totally dismayed, and said "Lily, you better look at it, and see it for yourself."

Lily assumed she had done a terrible job. She said "I never saw myself on TV."

And she sat in front of the screen and looked at it. When it was over she said "I like it, I think I did fine."

She was surprised but I knew she had done fine job.

So they said "do it again Lily, but this time don't drop your voice so often." I thought that was good direction. Dropping her voice didn't work, it took energy out of the story.

Lily said "Oh good! Direction! I want direction!"

So Lily did it again. Roy's cellphone rang in middle. It was just 5 musical notes, but he had her do that whole part again. And when it was over I realized Lily had left out one part which changed the meaning of what came next. And I would have liked that part to be done again. But Roy said "the light has changed, and there is not enough film left."

So the 3 of them got stoned on pot. And got into an hour long argument. I think Roy did not like it that the two women were talking to each other and ignoring him. Because as soon as he finished putting his camera away he said something very inflammatory. He said "Alice left the country and lived in Mexico for 25 years and then came back and she should not have been allowed back and had her citizenship taken away from her. Because for 25 years all her productive work had gone to Mexico not to USA."

I thought the idea was ludicrous, and especially senseless since clearly Roy and Alice are friends and collaborate together. How can Roy say Alice should not have been allowed to return home when he enjoys collaborating with Alice artistically now. He is saying something he does not mean.

But both girls really went for it. They got in passionate argument and their feelings got involved. After that all Roy did was land more incendiary bombs, and the girls went for it like a shot. And by the time we went in to eat Lily refused to talk to Roy.

We sat at Alice's round table in kitchen, even tho it had been so nice sitting outside her studio on steps in sunshine as Sun was going down. It was totally nice sitting there under the sky except for the senseless argument going on around me.

Alice's house was like those tenement apartments back in East Village in Manhattan. Maybe that is why it felt so comfortable and familiar. Her house is very homey. We sat at round table in her kitchen and ate Alice's delicious food and fresh arguments started up again.

And then Lily drove me back to the club where I was to meet Bill. In the car ride back to club, Lily had a lot to say about Roy. I think Roy was attracted to Lily, and Lily said she had made it clear to him she was not interested. I had found it amusing that Roy had joined Access TV because his friends had told him it was a way to meet hot young babes. Roy is 44. But clearly Roy would never have carried on this way with both Alice and Lily (around my age) if he didn't want both of them. And when Lily had said something about Janey coming, Roy was on it like a flash. "Who is Janey? Why didn't you bring Janey!" Seems to me Roy likes Alice, he likes her friend Lily, and he wanted Lily's friend Janey to meet too.

The next day I got phone call from Alice saying Roy had acted so obnoxious after we left she had to send him home. And also he told her if she doesn't have sex with him, he won't give her the videotape he made of Lily's reading, and she had said "I am not a whore."

So now we all have to meet Friday at the TV studio and do it again. Even tho Lily only has 20 minutes because it is her lunch hour.

Adventure at Access TV

I went down and did the show for Alice yesterday. Seems to me everything which could go wrong did go wrong. And when I got back home when it was all over I wrote email to Alice apologizing for screwing it all up.

However when I got up from my chair to go in and watch *Forbidden Planet* my Higher Self said she is pleased as punch with how everything went. So there are two opposite views on this, mine and hers. I was heavily influenced by Alice who said when I finished, "you held the paper in front of your face the whole time" and she looked at me appalled. How my Higher Self can say "it all went perfectly" beats me, but of course it is very sweet to hear.

Bill and I left at 10:30 am to go to Office Depot to pick up the booklets I had made of 4 of my stories, then we went to pool so I could swim a little, and then we arrived at Access

TV studio in downtown Tucson.

After I picked up the booklets and paid for them, I spent most of the trip on way to pool wondering why each one had cost 10 dollars. But my Higher Self kept saying, "forget about the money, you are going to be on tv, you want to be in happy frame of mind." And eventually I was able to put it out of my mind.

When we arrived at pool Bill said "it is already 11:30 and Alice's thing begins at noon, you can only swim for five minutes."

I said "but Bill, Alice told Lily it will take her an hour to set up the lights, that is why it is fine for Lily to arrive during her lunch hour."

But Bill insisted we arrive on time, so I shortened my swim. I had found an email from Lily just before we got up to leave, saying "I am very sorry Anne but I won't be able to make it after all, it just feels too rushed to me, so you read the story, you will do fine."

I took short swim, showered, put on dress, and we got in car to drive over there. There was a lot of construction on Stone Road, which was the cross street for downtown. But we both tried to be patient as traffic was at standstill.

We parked in Access TV studio parking lot. And Bill

said he was going to the Main Library, he didn't want to come up, so we arranged he would ask his Higher Self when I was finished, and we would meet in coffee shop across the street.

Alice came down with a woman to help her bring her paintings upstairs just as Bill and I were saying goodbye. And I figured that woman was another one of the artists Alice was going to do a half hour show on.

Alice looked beautiful, I've never seen her look so beautiful. Her hair was long and lovely with one side swept back with jeweled barrette. She had a long skirt made of all different patchwork designs, silk, but figure hugging. So it looked like one of those bustle skirts women wore at turn of century, except for the outstanding color and design. And a kind of black velvet jacket for top. She looked like a knock-out.

I went upstairs to Studio A. It is a huge room with many cameras high up. Alice was there, the woman artist I had seen downstairs, a man and a woman. Alice introduced me to the two women. I had thought both the women were artists going to do their shows for Alice, but the younger one, Evelyn, turned out to be a cameraman too. So was the young man. Just the woman (Delfina) was an artist waiting to do her show.

The young woman (Evelyn) was wearing a dress as if she was in a renaissance fair. The woman artist (Delfina) was wearing tailored clothes and pretty necklace. I didn't catch the name of the young man.

They were all involved in setting up Delfina's paintings and arranging them so the light would be right on them, and then setting up all the other lights.

I sat in a chair in the corner by myself. Delfina was talking to everyone. They all seemed to recognize her. Finally she came over to me and began talking to me. She said "I had that operation, I had had so many operations, and after that last one a few months ago, Carl came to take care of me. It was thought I was going to die and he would live, but it turned out the reverse, 3 days later he died. And that was several months ago. I am fine, but I am not going to have any more operations. But my memory isn't as good because I am so surprised to find that I am alive and he is not."

She said all this to explain why there was something she could not remember. I hadn't planned to get involved in socializing before the show, I wanted to keep my focus, but I actually understood what she was telling me.

Because back in NYC my friend Marjorie had told me, "I never planned to live past 30, so now I don't know what to do with my life." I told Delfina what my friend Marjorie said, and she was into it. She was happy someone understood her own experience.

Then she went back to help them light the paintings, and she was happy talking about her paintings with them. And I began to realize this was going to take a very long time.

She and I had now been there a whole hour and nothing had progressed as far as I could see. And I figured she would do her show first. I had waited an hour, and was now looking at waiting two more hours.

And I put my face in my hands. It was so uncomfortable sitting there. I don't mind empty time if I can lounge myself and communicate with my Higher Self. But to just sit uncomfortably on a chair, and have to go downstairs and outside each time I wanted a cigarette, and the wait seemed long, especially since there was no end in sight.

I was starting to get unhappy. Delfina walked over when I had my face in my hands, and said "I know just how you feel."

I said "is this thing ever going to happen?" and she said, "I don't know."

I was so surprised and touched she identified and understood that I said "I love you." I realized she had come over to pierce thru my unhappiness and I made huge effort to become happy.

After that I eavesdropped when she talked to the others. It seems Carl was her husband, and had been State's top Prosecuting Attorney, then Chief Justice of Arizona Supreme Court. He had many interesting cases, and the young man wanted to ask her about them. He said "tell me about Angela Davis, I've heard her name but I never knew what she did."

And Delfina said "that was a very interesting time" and "Angela Davis had been framed."

"It was all a frame" she said. And she said how Angela Davis' brother had come into court with a bag, opened it up, took out a rifle and began shooting people.

And the man said "why was Angela Davis on trial for what her brother did?"

And Delfina said "it was all a frame."

Then another hour passed, and I was looking very down in the mouth again. So Delfina came over and told me when she was 17 years old and living in Tokyo she had rheumatic fever. The Tokyo doctor showed her the x-ray, and showed her how her heart was leaking, and said "you only have till age 21 to live."

And Delfina went home and got out her mom's medical books, her mother was a physician, and looked it all up, and sure enough she only did have few years to live. So she got an alarm clock and decided to live by the clock. 15 minutes for this, 15 minutes for that, no regrets, no looking back, make each 15 minutes count.

She said the result is, she has had a very unusual life. And when she tells people about her life, she discovered no one believes her, they don't believe the things she said she did, she really did.

Again I understood what she was telling me, because of Alice. Alice's life is like no other life, and each time Alice tells me about her life, I have a hard time believing it, but I am learning now it is all true, and it all did happen, she just happened to have had a totally unusual life.

Delfina said "when I discovered no one believed me I stopped telling them about my life, but I decided 'who cares what others think.' I tell about my life because how else can I remember it all." I didn't tell Delfina why I understood what she was saying, but I think she realized I did.

She said she studied Oriental painting because she was in the East. And then she studied painting with the Indians. She said "Oriental painting is very interesting, they have a whole other way of painting."

And then she told me China had invited both her and Carl to live there. "You can live wherever you want" they told her. They wanted Carl to teach law there and for her to teach—

"Painting" I guessed.

"No, they didn't know I was painter, they wanted me to teach speech and theatrics." I don't know if she and Carl took up the job offer, but I do think they were taken all over China on guided tours.

Then there was another long wait. I was starting to get uncomfortable and unhappy again. It was now 2 pm and I couldn't take it. I still didn't see any progress. Delfina's show looked complicated, I figured she would go first, and it would be another two hours.

I said to Alice "I am leaving, I will be back at 4 pm."

And Alice said "Don't go! We will do you first because you are only 15 minutes and Delfina's show is complex."

So I said "OK."

So about 15 minutes later she had me and Delfina sit on

the stage to try out the lighting. And I thought "at last the show is on its way."

But it was another 45 minutes of us just sitting on the stage while they tried out the lighting. Each time we started to get impatient, they said "this is so you will look beautiful and glamorous, we are doing all this for you."

As I said to Delfina on the stage, "they appeal to our vanity, they say 'just be patient, we're doing this to make you beautiful.'"

And Delfina said "and it works!"

And I burst out laughing.

"Yes" I said "it works, we'll sit forever in order to look beautiful on tv."

I caught a glimpse of myself on the screen and got upset. I told Delfina "I have not looked in the mirror for 20 years, because each time I see myself in the mirror it ruins my whole day."

And Delfina said, her too, she never looks in the mirror.

"Why have your whole day ruined?" I said to Delfina.

"Exactly" Delfina said to me. And we both agreed we would not watch the show when it came on tv.

"Why ruin our life" I said.

And Delfina said "exactly."

I felt immensely close to Delfina sitting on the stage with her, both agreeing how we won't look in the mirror and we won't watch our show, because we don't like how we look.

"I will pray we both look like beautiful goddesses" I told Delfina.

"Thank you" she said.

I was going to tell Delfina to take off her glasses, but I thought maybe she doesn't want to. But we were up there so long that finally Delfina said, "I am going to take off my glasses, I only need them to read my poem, I'll put them back on then."

"Good idea" I said "Delfina, because your eyes have a sparkle to them."

And I have to admit sitting next to Delfina up on that stage for that 45 minutes while they did the lighting, the joy and beauty of the sparkle in Delfina's eyes, really lit me up.

I don't know how to describe it, it's as if a star in the night sky was greatly greatly greatly magnified, so all you saw was huge sparkle.

And that's really the story of the show. Delfina and I were up there holding hands the whole time to give each other support. When I was finally allowed to start I didn't waste any time because I really wanted to do this thing already.

I launched instantly into my story with my hand on Delfina's thigh, I had my left hand pressed on her thigh, with my right hand I read my story, I only took my hand off to flip the pages.

They said "don't look at the camera" so I looked at the clock. But each time I started a new part I looked into Delfina's eyes. And that huge loving sparkle of love and joy, sparkled, bigger than any star, with love and joy for me. Delfina turned it into heaven for me.

When it was over Alice came up and said "you had the page in front of your face the whole time," and she looked dismayed. I know I had made some mistakes. I had taken one part out of the story to read on tv, that I decided I wanted in when I discovered it wasn't there. So I had stopped myself from reading the final two paragraphs in the middle of reading it, got out my booklet I had made in xerox store, and read that part, and then went back and read last two paragraphs. I know it was weird.

But Alice looked totally dismayed about the whole thing. I had figured something wasn't going exactly right when I felt people leave the room and talk. I knew Alice and some of the others who worked there had left the room to say something I was doing was wrong. I didn't know it was because of the paper in front of my face. They should have had a table to put my story on.

Then I got off the stage and Alice got on to interview Delfina, and her show was starting. And a woman in the back of the room, I guess she had arrived to do her show, said "I like your dress."

And I said "your outfit is beautiful and that necklace." She was wearing the most beautiful African outfit, she could be the cover of a magazine.

She said "the children made this necklace, it is play dough, and my friend said 'wear it with your costume, it goes.'" It is a stunning costume, she will look glorious on tv.

I went downstairs and there was Bill. And I said "come on up, Alice prepared all this delicious Turkish food for everyone, it is all your favorite dishes."

So Bill said "let me lock up the truck."

And the Green Room had lots of pizza and all of Alice's food she had worked so hard to prepare. I had pizza and Bill had both. He had wanted to eat in an Arab restaurant and was so happy to find all these Middle Eastern dishes.

And then Delfina joined us in the Green Room, I guess her show was finished. And a lovely woman named Miriam arrived to do her show, she is writer too. And Miriam and Delfina began to talk.

I said to Delfina "you saved me."

And Delfina said "I was very nervous myself, but seeing you through your nervousness totally relaxed me, by the time I did my show I was completely relaxed."

"We saved each other" I said.

"Yes" Delfina said.

Alice edits my video

I hadn't seen Alice since we did the show together. But last week I saw her at the pool.

"I began editing your video" she said, "it is only 15 minutes."

"So put it on with Delfina's" I said, "that will make a half hour, and you have half hour show."

"I will" she said, "but it means taking 4 minutes out of Delfina's, maybe I will take out the poem she read."

Alice said "I edited out all the stuff from your video which shouldn't be there, I took out the part where you were naked."

"I was naked?" I said, "I don't remember that."

"And I took out the part where your dress fell down."

"My dress fell down? I don't remember that."

"And I edited out the part where you discovered a

part of your story you wanted in, wasn't in the pages you were reading, so you stopped, and said 'I want this' and found it on the table and read it from that."

I have problems with accuracy myself, but never would I have called pushing my bra strap back up 3 times, to I was naked, and my dress fell down.

Old Forge

Just as Mildred was my dad's favorite sister, her sons were my favorite cousins when I was growing up. Richie was exactly my age, we were best friends, and Alan was only two years younger, he could be included in our play. And even tho my little brother was 5 years younger then me, Richie nicknamed him Guchie and included him too.

Every Sunday we drove over to their apartment in Jackson Heights, where the two sets of parents had coffee and cake together, and the 4 of us played together. We always had a wonderful time.

And in the summers we were all up in Old Forge together. On beach days we all were at the beach together and I played with Richie in the water. But mountain summers don't have that many beach days, half the week is always cold and cloudy and rainy. I would walk over to

Richie's house in my raincoat and boots and we'd lie on his bed and read comic books and then walk over to the drug store for a phosphate, and visit the dogs in the neighborhood, there was a collie I liked a lot.

I loved our summers in Old Forge but Richie didn't. He said "it is boring, there is nothing to do," he had far more fun with his friends back in Jackson Heights. Life only got interesting for him when he sent away in the comic book for that Daisy BB gun, and set up the targets outside, and shot at them with his gun. We were best friends then and of course he offered to take turns with me and I tried.

But the BB gun didn't do anything for me, and it did everything for Richie. I guess it marked the end of our friendship because after that all he wanted to do was play with his BB gun, and it just didn't hold my interest. A girl named Nina arrived with her family to rent the house next door, and after that I spent all my time with Nina.

Richie and I had done a lot of things together before the BB gun arrived. We would fish together off the pier, we would go in the canoe together, he would take the back, I would take the front. And we would plan when we had real money to buy a motorboat together. He said he will have money when he has his Bar Mitzvah and I said I will have money when I have my Sweet 16.

I really don't know why I was so completely content up in Old Forge and Richie was so bored. When he said he had so much more fun with his friends back in Jackson Heights, I just took his word for it. I mean I assumed he had far more fun with his friends back in the city than I had with my friends.

But I wonder now if that was true. I visited Richie and Alan as kid, and sure it was fun throwing water balloons out the window on people, and flipping baseball cards, and playing fort with his friends downstairs in the trees around the apartment building.

But I was a jump-rope freak, what more fun is there than jump rope with all your friends! And we played Skelsy, and Girls & Boys, and over-the-knee, and Jacks, and Chinese handball and stickball and Potsy, and the box with the marbles game. We had a lot of good games too.

When I was very young in Old Forge I played with the Dennises across the street. They had so many kids, that playing with one family meant we could play all our games, thrilling games of Hide and Seek and Kick the Can. And Richie and Alan had the Beckinhams, with 10 kids, next door to them, as well as Dolphie in the big house, so they had kids to play with too.

I just liked our routine in Old Forge, I didn't miss my NYC life when I was up there at all. I found it totally fulfilling to be there. I would wake up and get out my bike and ride my brother on the back fender, and ride into town for jelly donuts. I loved jelly donuts.

The lady who worked in the bakery of D and D who sold us the jelly donuts was Floanne Wormwood's mother. She and Floanne lived in a trailer not far from us and I was friends with Floanne.

When my dad woke up he would build the fire in the pot belly stove, mountain mornings are cold. And when my mom put up the hot cereal, he and I would take long walk together while the cereal was cooking. We would walk down the road to where Floanne's trailer was and the other trailers, and then take the path behind it thru the woods, and walk on that path as long as we wanted to. It was probably a logging road, the Adirondacks is filled with logging roads. And we would chat and then come home for hot cereal.

When I was even littler, his favorite walk was to Charlie Able's farm. To get there we walked right on Route 28 in front of our house, there was a kind of footpath next to it, no sidewalks. And we'd pass about 4 houses. And just before the big fancy stone house which belonged to the principal, was Charlie Able's farm. We'd walk up the long winding road to reach it. And my dad loved talking to Charlie Able, and I got to have my one and only experience of a farm. I got to see the baby pigs and the chickens and everything. I loved it.

And my dad loved Charley Able. A rose bush grew up in front of our house which had the most beautiful smelling roses there was, pretty pink roses with a fragrance to die for. And Leon always said he must have picked up the seeds on his shoes when he was visiting Charley Able, that was his explanation of the roses. He loved those roses. And when I went away to camp he would always include one in the letter he sent me, and it would still have its miraculous perfume even if it had lost its beauty.

After that I would put on my swimsuit underneath my dungarees and flannel shirt and head to the beach. Because Maurice Dennis, the father of the kids across the street, was the beach lifeguard back then, and he gave swimming lessons in the early morning. And I wanted to earn those Red Cross cards.

I took Beginners with him, I took Elementary, I took

Intermediate Swimming. I earned card after card. And then the big day came when I was allowed to take Junior Life Saving which was my passion back then.

We had an eat-in glass porch. Which meant there was table there to look out at the woods and field, and 4 burner hotplate with small black stove sitting on top of it, my mother did all her cooking on that. The field was adjacent to our house but where our house ended the woods began. And my father would sit and have his meals there and watch the deer come out of the forest.

Or his favorite, watch the humming birds alight on the field wildflowers. He loved both. There would be hush when he would espy the deer arriving, and his thrilled joy at the humming birds. When the sun was actually warm and if it was sunny day, my mother would put up roast chicken in the little black oven on top of the hotplate, and we'd all set off for the beach.

I was allowed to buy jelly donuts for me and my brother in the early morning in town because my mission was to buy the New York Times for my father. He did not like to go one day without reading his New York Times and he had arranged with one of the drug stores to have one put aside for him each morning. So I would waltz in with my brother and ask for my father's New York Times and they would give it to me. My brother and I ate our jelly donuts right away, I discovered jelly donuts up in Old Forge. And then arrived home with Leon's New York Times.

It was on one of these excursions home with the New York Times in the basket of my bike and my brother on the back fender, that we bumped into my father's friend from New York, Vicky. She was older than even my father's big sister Esther. She was the doyenne of all the school teacher families from New York. And she said "did you hear the great news the war is over!"

I realize now she was referring to the Korean War, but at the time it didn't mean anything to me. I wasn't even aware there was a war, I wasn't even aware what war was. I was in a world of jelly donuts and swimming lessons. She was beside herself with joy and excitement and happiness, and I tried to chime in. But I don't know if I even mentioned it to my parents when I got back home, it simply didn't register. All that registered was that Vicky had talked to me as if I was a grown up. Saying "great news the war is over" seemed like grown up talk to me.

My mother set up our beach blanket next to the other families from NY, and I looked for Richie and we went into the water together and played games in the water. And I guess my father headed straight for the tennis court and played tennis. And we all had glorious time.

Until my mom said "time to go home for dinner." In Old Forge we had our meals differently. We had dinner at lunch. When we arrived home the roast chicken was already roasted, the apple pie she had made from apples in the backyard was already baked, and we had our delicious meal on our eat-in porch. And that is when my father would see the deer or the humming birds.

Then we would return to the beach and it was the long wait of one hour before we were allowed to go back in the water. Old Forge was so far north, evening did not start till quite late. So there was time for endless afternoons. Richie and I played in the water, walked up to Rudy's for ice cream cones, collected empty bottles, brought them to Rudy's for two cents each and bought candy with it, and we played a lot of cards. The men all sat on one big blanket and played Hearts.

And when we had changed out of our bathing suits and back into shorts and tops again, the serious tennis playing began. All my aunts and uncles played tennis, they played doubles with each other. But my father was the best tennis player of all and long after all my cousins and aunts and uncles had gone home, my brother and I would sit on the bench, I guess my mom was there too, and my father would play with all the best tennis players in the neighborhood.

There was one young man who would come from up the Channel on his motor boat to play with Leon every evening. He was a great tennis player too. And my brother and I sat there for long endless beautiful match. It was how tennis got into our blood. Love ten, Love twenty, Deuce, all the names, we knew them by heart. Set, match, serves, backhands.

My father taught both of us how to play tennis as soon as we could hold a tennis racquet. Each time he got a new racquet he gave his old one to my mom, who gave her old one to me, and I gave my old one to my brother. Back then you had to keep your tennis racquet in a press with screws, and sometimes I got a good enough one from my mother that I had to do that too. I knew all about tennis racquets and which were the best ones. We would play as a family if no one else wanted the courts.

Sometimes instead of watching my dad play tennis, my mom would take me and my brother in the car to go buy the chicken and eggs from the egg lady. That was a nice drive in a different direction, around the lake, up and up a windy road, and we would come to some house. And she would ask for her capon and her two dozen eggs.

Supper was simple. I was allowed to go to the movies once a week. There was a movie theater just before you hit the center of town. I used to take the short cut in the field beside it when I was visiting Richie. Outside the movie theater were the movie posters. And I would study them to make my choices. The other night *Shane* came on TV, and I remembered when I had stood outside that movie theater and the poster from *Shane* had been up, and how long and hard I had looked at it trying to decide if that would be my choice.

The movies changed on Saturday, Sunday was different movie, I could only see one. I did miss *I Love Lucy* my favorite show, when I was up there, we had no TV, and when the movie poster showed *Long Long Trailer* with Lucy and Ricky, of course I chose that. The other choice was Danny Kaye movie *The Court Jester.* But for me there was no competition with Lucy. I chose *Long Long Trailer* and went to see it. It was not good. The next evening my parents went to see the Danny Kaye movie, and my mother loved it so much she broke the rule for me. She said "you can see it too even tho you already went to the movies." And I loved it. I had felt very gypped that the one I had chosen turned out to be a lemon and the one I had not chosen was so great.

Danny and Sarah, one of the couples up there as New York City school teachers, knew how to lead folk dancing, so once a week, in some huge long log cabin affair, officially called the hay fever center, with an old cannon from the revolutionary war in front of it with plaque, Danny and Sarah held folk dancing. First all the children had folk dancing. Then the grown ups. Sometimes we stayed to watch the grown ups dance, most of the time my brother and I were sent home to bed.

I had no idea that after the folk dancing the grown ups would walk across the street to the beach, take off their clothes and swim naked in the lake, until one morning my mom told me "we were all swimming naked in the water, and when we wanted to come out and get dressed, there were teenagers on the swings, and we couldn't get out of the water until they left, and they would not leave."

There was bingo in the Fire House once a week which I loved too.

And then Chuck who worked in the Post Office told me he was opening up a miniature golf course, and of course once that happened life really took off. I fell in love with miniature golf, I loved it. It was open every night and they sold popcorn there too. It was high up, on top of the big hill across from the Fire House, and all thru August we would watch the shooting stars as we played miniature golf. My cousins did that too, I played with Richie. And I learned to see the Big Dipper and the North Star and the Little Dipper too.

And some mornings instead of beach, or maybe when it was too cold and cloudy for beach, my mother took us all near the ski slopes to go huckleberry picking. I always think of huckleberries in hot dry dusty places, but there is no way we would be huckleberry picking instead of at the beach unless it was not beach weather.

And on Wednesday mornings she took all the cousins horseback riding in Thendara, which I loved too. Richie's horse was Daisy, a pinto. And I rode Freckles. I don't know which horse my brother rode. I remember my mom rode Dexter, he was chestnut.

Mrs. DuBois ran the riding stable and CarolAnn who lived across the street was her assistant. CarolAnn was my age and we became friends, and she taught me games to play with horses. How you can slide off backwards, like on a slide. You just slide down their tail, it was fun.

My dad once took home movies of me sliding off the horse that way, but for some reason it was at night, the movies are too dark to see. If I hadn't known what I was doing in them I wouldn't have known. But there is CarolAnn and me and my horse and my climbing up again and again for the fun of sliding off. I wonder now what the horse thought, but I guess he found it fun playing with two joyous little girls.

Because it rained so much up there, many many afternoons I put on my raincoat and boots and walked into town to the library. It was right next to the movie theater. There was a wonderful librarian there. As soon as I walked in she would say "I know just what you would like" and she would pick out ten books for me, and they were all heaven.

My father had paid Maurice Dennis to remodel the house one winter, to put in a knotty pine kitchen, and a little bedroom next to it so I could have my own room, and have the little bedroom painted pink the color I wanted. Before that I shared a bedroom with my brother on the second floor next door to the bathroom and my parent's bedroom. I loved my little pink bedroom on the ground floor. There was a little brass bed in there. I would lie in bed and practice my scissors kick for Intermediate Swimming, that is when you are taught the side stroke. But mainly I would read.

Yes I found *The Saturdays* all on my own in the Pomonok library near our house in Flushing and I discovered it was a series and I read all of them. And I think I discovered *Dr Doolittle* in Queens too and read all of them, that was a huge favorite.

But the librarian in Old Forge introduced me to everything. I read *Black Beauty* because of her, and *Bambi,* and a book about a whale where the whale describes his whole life thru the seas, that was an amazing book.

I read so many books from the point of view of animals that she found me. I even read a book about the adventures on a submarine, the only book my cousin Richie took out too. I don't think we had the same taste in books but he and I both liked that wonderful adventure book of the submarine.

I am sure she found *Mary Poppins* for me. I had read a chapter from *Caddie Woodlawn* in my reader in school and loved it, and she showed me they had *Caddie Woodlawn* there and I read the book and loved it. And she introduced me to *Little House on the Prairie* and I loved them all.

And several months ago when I was wondering what a perfect life in Heaven meant, and I tried to think about a perfect life— how I wanted to have everything I have in Tucson, my beautiful desert, and everything I loved in Old Forge, a lake and docks and trees. And I thought about all the people I wanted to be friends with, I remembered that wonderful librarian in Old Forge and wanted her to be my friend too.

How it all started

I had dropped out of college when I was 20, and I went to look for a job. I went to The American Museum of Natural History and called on the house telephone to Lew. My friend from college, Pam, had worked for him on a fellowship from NSF. And she had brought him home for dinner. He seemed like a nice man, but I had been too shy to notice. I was intimidated a grown up was in the house, but he was nice for a grown up. I called him on the house telephone and said "Dr. Irizarri, I am Anne, Pam Holder's friend, you had dinner at our house, I am looking for a job."

And he said "stay right there, Anne, I am coming down, you are an answer to a prayer." And he came down and told me he was just wishing he had 25 extra hours a week to do the things he wanted, and since he didn't have them, he wanted a Girl Friday to do them for him, and he had no idea about how to go about finding a Girl Friday, and he hired me on the spot.

Then I called my mother. "I decided to drop out of college for one semester" I told her.

"But what will you do" she said.

"I will get a job" I said.

"But who will ever hire you" she said.

"Dr. Lewis Irizarri, anthropologist at The American Museum of Natural History just did" I told her.

That was a wonderful job and Lew turned out to be the loveliest employer I ever had as well as a great friend who has lasted me my whole life.

Lew made a lot of things possible for me. Above all he gave employment to me any time I needed a job, which made possible the changes I was making in my life.

It caused a huge commotion at home when I decided to drop out of college, even tho I told them it was just for one semester. When my mother said "what will you do" it shut her right up that I said Lew had hired me. After all I was working at the American Museum of Natural History for an anthropologist, a curator of ethnology. Their whole idea of college was so it would give me a job. And the job I had for Lew sounded good on paper. Or should I say, where I was working and who I was working for, sounded very good on paper. They had no idea what my actual job was. They probably thought I was a research assistant.

"Annie dropped out of college" my dad told his sisters.

"O no!" they said, "what will she do."

"She is working for an anthropologist at the American Museum of Natural History, she is his research assistant."

"O that doesn't sound too bad" they said.

It sounded like a job I would get when I had gotten my degree, before I became a school teacher like everyone else in the family.

I was living at home then. And I would get dressed each day and take the bus and 3 subway trains to the Museum. My job was 5 hours a day. I would arrive at the Museum and Lew would make a list of what he wanted. And I would set out to do it. A friend of Lew's and mine at the Museum, a nice girl from Wisconsin, used to refer to my job as "are you still doing Lew's shopping for him?" Which was an accurate description of my job, altho Lew and I both preferred calling it, I was his Girl Friday.

My first assignment was to go to Madison Square Gardens and get their schedule of their college basketball games. I was told to make sure it is the college games. Then he sent me to the 42nd Street Library to look up zip codes of some people he was writing to in Maine. It was all on a list. So I went from one place to another. I realize now everything Lew had me get for him or look up for him, people no longer hire a Girl Friday to do that for them, it is all on internet.

But I went to Madison Square Garden and got him the schedule of the college basketball games, I went to the ticket office. Then I walked over to the 42nd Street Library and looked up all the things he wanted me to look up. And then I walked along 5th Avenue and window shopped, and I think I bought myself a pair of shoes. And he wanted a large box of Kleenex and I bought that for him. And in all my long time of working for him, it was the only error I ever made. It turns out when Lew had written Kleenex down on the paper he meant Kleenex. I had bought tissues. Kleenex pops up. I had to exchange it.

Then because he was a member of the faculty at Columbia University, or something, he had library privileges there. He was allowed to take out books. And he had a long list of books he wanted. That was the only assignment which was a little hard, carrying all those books back to the Museum. I guess I took the bus, but still I had to walk to the bus stop with them and then walk to the Museum.

All my jobs were variations on the above it seems to me. I kept track of my own hours, and Lew paid me 50 dollars a week for 25 hours. I felt like I got the best of the bargain because I would do long window shopping and shopping on way back to the Museum. And I was astounded years later, when Lew had had a slew of Girl Fridays who followed in my footsteps, when he told Janet, I was the best of all of them. Janet said his newest one is always lying down in the ladies room at the Museum.

Pam and Ellie had worked for Lew on a Fellowship. Ellie and Lew remained best friends, she would visit us in the office. Ellie was my age, so when June came, she graduated Hunter College, and my assignment for that day was to buy all the stuff so we would have party for Ellie in the office. I thought "this sure is a neat job, going to work means buying the candy and cake and having a party with Ellie in the office."

A few months after I began working for Lew, one of my boyfriends, Alan, returned home from Italy, and was staying at his parents' house in Queens. He called me up and said "I have decided to write a novel and I think you would be easy to live with while I write my novel, do you want to share an apartment with me in the East Village?"

I had a big crush on Alan then. I think he had other girlfriends. He said he chose me because "you won't bother me while I am writing." And I accepted the offer even tho it was hardly an expression of passionate love. It had been my dream for long time to live with a guy.

I didn't know what the East Village was, I had never lived there, I had always lived with roommates on the Upper West Side of Manhattan while I had been in college. But Alan picked me up, and we found an apartment on East 12th Street between A and B. So I told my parents, "I am moving into an apartment with Sue Pruitt." She had been my friend from City College and come home one evening for dinner, and my brother and father were smitten with her, such a beautiful blond, and my mom liked her too. I said "Alan is helping me move my stuff," and she said "OK." And I moved in with Alan on East 12th Street.

I completely forgot my parents thought I was living with Sue Pruitt, till one night, when I was in bed with Alan, two young men knocked on the door. I could hear them from the other side of the wall. And one was a friend from college.

He said "Anne, your mother gave me your address, and I am here with my friend Steve, to take you and Sue out."

I don't think I opened the door. I called thru the wall, "I am not living with Sue, I am living with Alan." And they went away. I had had a crush on him in college and he had never responded, and I thought "wow if you wait long enough he did ask me out." But it was too late, I was living with Alan now.

Also I realized how much my mom believed I was living with Sue, if she directed the two young men to my apartment so they could take us out on a date.

My mom decided to visit me at the Museum with her new best friend Nicole from Cairo, Egypt. They were both going for their Masters in Public Health at Columbia together. Lew was very gracious to both the women and I took them around, and showed them everything on the 5th floor where the public is not allowed to go. And I also confided to my mom I am not living with Sue, I am living with Alan and I am very happy. Which caused total apoplexy. She had a fit and her whole visit was ruined.

"Why are you so upset" I kept saying, "I am happy, that is all that matters."

"That is not all that matters" she kept saying.

"If you love him why don't you marry him" she said.

"I don't want to get married, I like living with him."

She was very upset about it.

When I walked with Nicole alone I said "I don't know why she is so upset."

I was now 21. I had moved in with Alan month before my 21st birthday. I liked my life at the time. I loved living with Alan in the East Village (we became close after we began living together; he proposed marriage). I loved the East Village, I loved working for Lew at the Museum.

Alan was working for his dad. His dad had an attaché case factory on Broom Street. Alan worked in the office. He had all those beautiful clothes he had bought in Rome. And each morning we had breakfast, and then wore very attractive clothes. I was wearing very pretty nylon stockings then, with nice shoes, nice skirt, nice blouse. Maybe Alan wore a suit, and he had an attaché case of course. And we set off for the subway together. Alan had developed the habit of drinking tea when he was in Rome, so we had tea for breakfast. But my craving for coffee had not left, so after I left Alan I stopped at coffee shop for cup of coffee and donut, and then took subway up to the

Museum.

And Alan introduced me to pot. I don't know if I would have smoked it, if I wasn't just starting to live with him, and still had huge crush on him, and wasn't yet comfortable in his company. I was trying to please him. So it was a toss up, my reluctance to "take a drug" or my desire to please him. And my desire to please him won. I took the drug, I was willing to try pot. And almost instantly—maybe not the first time or the second time when nothing happened, but the third time when I got high— it was a great love affair. It was a love affair which ended very badly, but for a long time pot was a huge joy in my life.

It was my first experience of liberation. I just didn't know I could have that. To be free to be myself. And to actually experience my own mind. I found my own mind thrilling, I loved it. And I loved being free to be myself. It was so much fun to be myself.

Nancy Cantor

I dreamt about Nancy Cantor all night. She was my first friend after college. I graduated college in August. I had to spend that extra summer studying for the finals I had not taken during finals week in June and doing term papers. It was a wild summer, the "Summer of Love". And I had sublet an apartment for the summer on the corner of St Mark's Place. My friend from college, Francine, roomed with me. I was stoned the whole summer and do not know how I managed to take those finals and write those papers. But by end of summer I did, and I got my degree. And then immediately found a job at The Riverdale Children's Agency.

I had gone down for that job because the year before Wendy had worked there. Sometimes I would meet her in Central Park during her lunch hour, right by the Agency, it was at 79th and Madison Avenue. Because Wendy worked there I thought it would be a nice place to work. So I interviewed and they hired me. The woman in charge, Mrs. Streeter, liked me in the interview and hired me. Olive Streeter, the name comes back to me now.

The weekend before I was going to start work, a friend I had been a camp counselor with 3 summers before, invited me to go swimming in Rye, New York, where his parents had their home and where he was staying for the summer. He picked me up in his car at St Mark's Place and First Avenue, and I must have worn my bikini under my sundress, because I remember taking off my dress in the car to show him my new bikini (it was my first bikini) and he said "will it stay up?"

Ken– his name was Ken– Ken Adler. I always felt very close to him because one of the times when he had invited me to his parents' house in Rye so I could swim in the bay there, we had been swimming and he said "Anne I have a cramp in my leg, I can't make it back to shore."

And I said "put your hands on my shoulders, I'll swim under you and swim you back to shore," which I did.

At dinner that night he told his parents, "Anne saved me, she rescued me in the water."

And they said "O really" and the conversation moved on. For all the huge drama which goes on in learning how to be a junior life saver when I was 11 years old, all the huge dramatic rescues I did when we took turns playing the victim, the one actual rescue I did was the quietest simplest thing which ever happened. I swam him to shore, he said "thank you," he told his parents at dinner, and it was clear nobody believed us, and that was that.

On my previous visits I had stayed in his big sister's room and it was a beautiful room. Their whole house was a mansion, which made visiting there so much fun for me. I loved swimming in the bay, I liked Ken Adler a lot, and I found it a lot of fun to stay in a mansion, and in the bedroom of this princess sister, it was a bedroom for a princess.

This was the last time I visited there. And on my last day the Princess herself arrived. I finally got to meet her, Margie Adler. And when Ken drove me back to the city, Margie was in the car with us. And when I mentioned I start work the next day at Riverdale Children's Agency, Margie turned to her brother and said "Isn't that where Nancy Cantor works?" Apparently a friend of Margie's named Nancy Cantor worked there and I got so excited.

I was thrilled with the fairy tale princess Margie. I barely knew her, just that car ride back to the city, but I had stayed in her princess bedroom 3 times. In my mind she was Princess Charming. So naturally I saw Nancy Cantor as an extension of her, it was the next best thing to being friends with Margie.

When I arrived the first morning I asked the girl at reception where you check in, "is Nancy Cantor here?" And she said "Nancy is on vacation, she will be back in a week." And I waited the whole week, and then sat by reception when the week was over, to wait for Nancy. Each woman who arrived, I thought "is that Nancy?" Finally one woman arrived and the woman at reception said "that is Nancy Cantor."

So I followed her up the steps, and said, "I am a friend of Margie Adler's, she told me you work here."

Nancy said "I just got back from Nantucket, I rode my bicycle everywhere, I am lost without my bicycle." That was our first conversation.

Nancy says now she tried to give me the brush-off because I had said I was friend of Margie Adler's and she couldn't stand Margie Adler. But I had waited a whole week to meet Nancy, I wanted to be friends with her, I did not notice her attempts at brush-off. Yes she seemed a little aloof, but I didn't know her then, whatever aloof things she did I assumed was part of how she was. It never crossed my mind I was being brushed off. I said "let's have lunch together."

Nancy took me to the Madison Avenue Pub which I loved. I had never eaten in a place like that before, I felt so sophisticated. The cheeseburger was scrumptious. And Nancy told me she lived a block away. She had a small apartment in a brownstone around the corner from Madison Avenue. Over lunch we totally hit it off. And Nancy and I remain best friends to this day.

Sometimes I had lunch with all the other girls who worked there, which was a lot of fun. I liked the place we all had lunch in, I would order a chocolate egg cream or vanilla egg cream with my lunch, and I loved all the girls, they were great. One of them even turned out to be the big sister of a girl who had been in the clique way back at Higley Hill. She was a very pretty girl and very popular girl. Even tho a beautiful Polynesian-princess-looking girl was the head of the clique, the boys actually chose Phyllis. They were all in love with Phyllis. And Nora turned out to be Phyllis' big sister. Altho Phyllis was tall and Nora was short. Nora was also very pretty.

Nora and I must have gone somewhere together at night, and we must have been stoned. Because I remember being in a car with her on 14th Street and I said to her "are you stoned?" And she said "why, am I driving badly?" and I thought, 'How do I know how someone is driving,' it never occurred to me to pay attention.

I felt close to Nora because if her sister had been in socialist camp with me it meant her parents were like my parents. Also I felt close to Nora because she told me her boyfriend used to be Melvyn Margolies. Melvyn Margolies was such a complete and total wild man, that even tho Nora seemed so lovely, so pretty, so elegant, so classy, how could she not be a fun natural girl with a boyfriend like that. It was impossible for me to picture them together. I could not see how any girl would go for Melvyn, he was way too wild.

There was another girl who worked there that I liked a lot. She was a blond. She also lived in the area. And during her lunch hour she would go home to walk and feed and pet her huge German shepherd and I went with her. She was devoted to her dog. She was such a nice girl.

She had a problem. The Riverdale Children's Agency

was a foster care agency, and many of the children were teenagers. Our job as social workers was to take them out to lunch, ask them how everything is going, and also sometimes to visit the foster home. But mostly to take them out to lunch or take them to nice things. My caseload had some teenaged girls and some children, but her caseload had some teenaged boys. And of course she was beautiful zaftig blond and a very nice person, so the teenaged boys were very attracted to her. They were young men and she was a beautiful blond.

I had a great time when we all went out to lunch together, but as soon as I became best friends with Nancy she and I went to Madison Pub together for cheeseburgers and talked. She liked me very much and invited me to her house around the corner, and soon we had sleepovers. I invited her to my apartment in the East Village and I took her to everything I went to. I took her to an early women's liberation meeting but that didn't work for Nancy. But I took her to The Pageant Players loft to watch them perform, and also to go to their workshops on Wednesday evenings. And she loved The Pageant Players.

We'd go back to my apartment after work. I'd take her to B&H, she loved the food. Then I would put on an outfit and get stoned, Nancy didn't smoke pot. And we'd take the bus to the Pageant Players loft on East Broadway. I remember once getting stoned with Nancy and seeing her with new eyes. "You pretend to be a Jewish social worker" I told her "but really you are Sophia Loren, an Italian actress." Which was astute of me, Nancy was a beautiful actress, and she is the most dramatic girl I ever met, she is thrilling.

Nancy loved the Pageant Players, and once she brought along her friend from Boston College or from Berkeley, Nancy had gone to both colleges. Her friend critiqued The Pageant Players, "the girls are not good but the boys are great." I was surprised at the critique because in my mind the Pageant Players were above criticism, they were a glorious amazing experience. Nancy's friend was like Nancy, and not a little hippie chick like me. She was even more stolid than Nancy. Nancy's stolidness was just a façade, underneath the girl was wild, just as wild as me, but her friend was not.

The first time I took Nancy to Pageant Players she had not known about the 7 flights you have to climb up to get to the loft, and they are long flights. But the next time she remembered.

We stood at the bottom of the steps and she said "I'm not climbing up all those steps." She refused to budge. I did not know what to do. However I was very stoned.

I said "Nancy, they moved down to the loft one flight below, it is not such a long climb."

So she said "OK." And when we reached the loft she said, "it's amazing, that one flight makes a big difference."

And I said "they did not move, I made it up."

Getting Nancy to leave for the Pageant Players wasn't that easy either. She had her supper at B&H and for dessert she ordered noodle pudding. When it was time to go to East Broadway, Nancy would say "I cannot move! O that noodle pudding!"

I was high as a kite and said "that's OK Nancy, I'll just ring for the elevator," and marched out the door. Which got her up in a flash, since I lived in a tiny walk-up and there was no elevator.

After we had been friends for a year Nancy said "I have discovered liberation, I stopped wearing my girdle." And I giggled to myself, because of course by this time I had stopped wearing a bra, I couldn't imagine Nancy had been wearing a girdle all this time. Who wears a girdle!

I loved sleeping over at Nancy's house. She would get

out negligees for us to sleep in. It was my first negligee, it was so much fun to wear a negligee. And she would make Rice Crispies with milk and sliced bananas for breakfast which I loved. And one time her old boyfriend from college visited and she cooked us roast lamb. I always had delicious food with Nancy. She took me to the Jewish Institute which was a few blocks from where we worked, and we would have delicious lunches there too. And it was Nancy who introduced me to Ideal Coffee Shop, which was a German restaurant on York Avenue, not far from where she lived. I never had German food before, it was so delicious.

The great thing about Nancy is she was always game, and we had great times together. When women's liberation was invited to a fancy banquet in the art museum in Philadelphia, I went with Jeannie and Ti-Grace, and I took Nancy. We met at Grand Central Station and we were late for the train. I charged down the steps and when I turned around to look for Nancy, I was appalled to see her slowly sailing down on the escalator. When she finally reached bottom she said "O Annie you flew! You should have seen your face when you saw me on the escalator."

Nancy had zero interest in women's liberation but she

loved adventure. Jeannie and Ti-Grace talked women's liberation politics the whole train ride, but Nancy's comment was about Ti-Grace. "She wears tiger-striped print dress, very low cut, over left breast she wears button 'Feminism' and her name is Ti-Grace which sounds like tigress. It is extremely provocative and seductive."

Lifeguard in stand at my Tucson swim pool

Part II My Tucson Life

My Trip to Patagonia Lake

The heat has abated a little. It is down to 97 in the afternoons. So the nights have been cooler again. Plus the cloud cover, which held the big heat two days ago, has abated too. So we got 3 treats at once. It was only 97. Without cloud cover the coolers were effective, I didn't sweat in house all afternoon. And it is huge treat to have cool night follow hot day. I woke up thinking "if only our whole summer were like this."

And I realized this is just what the summer is like in Patagonia, a teeny town, not far from Tucson which features a lake, which is why I have been there.

For a girl who spent every summer of her childhood at the start of the Fulton Chain of Lakes in the Adirondacks, I couldn't believe they called Patagonia a lake when we finally arrived there.

It was our 4th year in Tucson, I wanted to go to a lake. Bill got out a map, and found the closest one was Patagonia Lake. It was during monsoon season of summer. I remember the skies being filled with lightning on the whole drive home. The monsoons don't arrive till 4 pm, so it must have been late morning when we left.

It wasn't far distance, and Bill found a route which was pretty. I think instead of the huge highway, we went on Old Spanish Trail, which must have been the road before the huge expressway was built.

You pass a lot of desert, I bet most of that is filled in with housing developments now. And then it must become higher up because the landscape changes, the desert becomes more meadowier, and prettier to eyes who have just seen desert for long time.

It must have seemed enchanting to me because I thought "I wouldn't mind living here." Then we hit the town we had seen on the map, I forget its name, maybe Sonoita, and to my astonishment, it was a convenience store and that was it. That was the whole town. We stopped and I went in and got a sandwich and a big soda.

Of course it wasn't a regular convenience store, like one on every block in Tucson. When it serves a whole hub like that, it has to have everything everyone wants. It had home-made hero sandwiches, it had big video section, it had a lot. And it was busy. We had traveled thru horse country and wine country to reach it. We didn't pass any houses but I guess it was all ranches.

Then after that the mountain range to the East changed. It was a different mountain range and a very pretty one. You felt like you had seen it before in every cowboy movie you ever watched. And then there was a little town, a bona fide town, stretched out along the route. Not that long but long enough. I think there was even an Italian restaurant. And whole stretched-out town faced directly out at those beautiful mountains, in the most beautiful spot of the mountains. It took my breath away.

It was exactly what I had pictured looking out at, when I saw all those cowboy movies. The town facing those mountains like that, was exactly how I had pictured living out West to be. Here was the whole dream of living out West, the beauty I had pictured. At first I just assumed every cowboy movie ever made must have been made here. Else why was this view so familiar, so dear, so epitomizing for me, and exactly what I wanted.

Why else would I feel I have always known this and

now I have found it— here it is in the life, far more beautiful than I even pictured, but perfect in every detail.

The odd thing tho is now that I have been in Tucson 10 years longer, since we drove past that little town of Patagonia (that was its name) facing right into those beautiful mountains, I don't know if any cowboy movies were made there. Because it turns out the studio where all the cowboy movies were made is in Tucson. I have never been to Old Tucson Studios like everyone else has, but just outside of Tucson, right on our very own desert, is the huge tract of land, of desert, where all the cowboy movies were made.

And even *Shane* came on tv few months ago, that is one I saw in movie theater in full color as kid, where the beauty of the West was fully pictured, that wasn't made in Arizona, that is Colorado beauty. So the deep perfection and satisfaction of the beauty I gazed out at, as we passed Patagonia, "I found it! I found it! this is what I always wanted, this is where I want to live!" didn't come from any movie. I concentrated very hard as we passed the town, to see what the town had, because I knew one day I wanted to move there.

And right after we passed the town (town wasn't long,

maybe a mile or two miles, if that, a mile sounds right, maybe 50 establishments all told) for some reason it seemed to turn marshy or watery to the right.

Where that water came from I have no idea (there is no water on the desert).

Right after that, you enter what looks like a State Park parking lot. This is really a riot. Because there are huge State Park roads leading into it, as if you are arriving at Jones Beach on Long Island. Vast roads with major State Park signs about Patagonia Lake. And a whole set-up to pay or show your pass, with men and women in Forest Service uniform in booths. You think where you are arriving is such a big deal, and I assumed it would be. And then you arrive at the lake, and you think "they call this a lake!"

For anyone who comes from a world where there is water, it seems like such a joke to have traveled all this distance. Any one of their 3 well-maintained parking lots was far bigger than this "lake". I guess the lake is bigger than my back yard, but not by much.

I found out later it is a man-made lake, and you can excuse me if I scoff at man-made lakes. I know it is a big deal here on the desert, and I once was on a forum where a guy proudly told me his dad helped build Patagonia Lake. Of course they pretend it is a real lake. They had paddle boats for rent, maybe even canoes. And ropes for swimming area. And it was filled with families, and there were places to cook-out around the lake.

It had one nice feature, which was there were no rules.

My memory of lakes with lifeguards in lifeguard stands, is the rules. They don't let you swim past the ropes for swimming area. In Old Forge we had to wait till 6 pm when lifeguard left, to swim across the lake to shore on other side. But of course that was a real swim, thru deep water, a mile long.

And don't forget the huge Old Forge lake, it circled all the way around, it was a mile across at the edge where we sat and played and where the lifeguard was, and ropes for swimming, but after the dock, it continued on for big distance, and then led out into a Channel, which eventually took you to First Lake, and all the lakes in the Fulton Chain of Lakes.

The Old Forge lake wasn't even called a lake, it was officially designated a pond, because all the other lakes are vast. But compared to Patagonia Lake, the Old Forge Pond is vast.

Because there were no restrictions on where you were allowed to swim— why would there be, the water never went above your head— Bill and I swam across the lake and sat on the rocks there and watched the birds. Since no one else was there, I took off my suit in the water and I treaded water, while Bill sat on rock, and we chatted, and watched all the birds overhead. There were a lot. I guess because of the lake, they wanted water.

Then I put my suit back on underwater, and we swam back to the swimming area, where I chatted with a teen-age girl. She told me she lives in Sierra Vista. I have the impression most there were from Sierra Vista, it is very close to Sierra Vista. They have to come here to swim, Sierra Vista has no pools. It wasn't that they have no pool at all, but something very odd. Like only one pool and it is never open (she explained to me). It was the first time I realized that Tucson's abundance of municipal pools, is not a given everywhere else, in every other city on desert. We are fortunate and blessed to have what we have. Can you imagine having to drive to Patagonia Lake each time you wanted to swim.

Also the water was stagnant. At first I was glad to be back in a lake, and not a municipal swimming pool, where water has texture and you can smell that you are in a lake. But the texture was off, way too cloudy, and even the smell was off. It was the strong smell of stagnant water, rather than the lovely smell of fresh sweet water.

But what the heck! It was a Sunday. Everyone was having a great time in the lake and around the lake. I was allowed to swim across it, and took my suit off. Everyone seemed very happy there, and there weren't any rules. There were cookouts on the "beach."

I am surprised now at the full amount of freedom. People even had their dogs with them. I am stunned at all the freedom, because contrary to my expectations as a New Yorker, the West has no freedom.

There are huge vast wild mountain ranges all around Tucson, completely wild and empty, and filled with wild animals. But either the sign says "dog must be kept on leash at all times" or "no dogs allowed."

Of course this is some insane rule, because supposedly there are wild mountain sheep at the top, and supposedly dogs have bothered them. But that is enough for Tucson, or Forest Service, whoever makes the rules, to make rule to take away your freedom.

After living out West for 15 years I will now say the only

place which has any freedom is New York City. Every other place has a rule about everything or at least Tucson does.

Which is what made Patagonia Lake wonderful, there were zero rules, and everyone had a wonderful time there. It was perfectly happy atmosphere. Not much of a lake, but a happy place.

When it was time to leave I saw the lightning start over the mountains, so my Higher Self suggested we take a different route home, away from the storm. The threatened storm never did arrive but it sure looked like it would.

This route was not pretty. It was pretty finding it. We had to drive down to Nogales. This was a lot of fun, because you drive down all the mountain curving roads to reach Nogales. And because of my summers in Adirondacks, I am addicted to curving mountain roads. Also I am addicted to hills which you never see on desert. I loved driving down all the hilly curving mountain roads with houses on either side. All kinds of houses, not development houses, Nogales must be an old town.

Nogales is the city which is on the border of Mexico, so the houses were Mexican styled, which made them so pretty, and each one was different. It was fun to see. And set in (am I hallucinating this) woods and trees. Maybe we drove down the foothills of some mountain range.

Then we got on I-10 which is a 10 lane expressway, and I don't remember anything about that drive back, except hoping it would be over already. And then we entered the city limits of Tucson, and Tucson seemed very cityish after being out in the country. And that was the whole trip. I assumed it was the beginning of taking trips, but it turned out to be the first and last one I ever took. And now I have even forgotten about the idea of taking trips.....

Gene

It's not my favorite weather. But if you get up early enough, there is a kind of pearly beauty to the overcast desert. Clarity is gone, but all the green merges and shimmers. It doesn't quite merge, it's like an impressionist painting where nothing has definition. O a little birdie whistled. Now it whistled again. It is an encouraging sound.

Bill took me shopping yesterday which was a lot of fun. All the pretty skirts which used to be fifty dollars were now 10 dollars. I chose 3 and a pretty top to go with them, also an attractive zip sweatshirt for walking Lulu in winter. I am wearing the pretty top now. It is fun having a new top.

Then we went swimming at Fort Lowell pool. The water is deep there but it was warm as bathwater. I didn't care. Their clock broke and they haven't replaced it but I noticed the lifeguards are on 15 minute shifts. After 4 shifts I went and took my shower.

I had bought magenta nail polish the day before, and it was fun painting my fingernails and toenails after my shower this pretty shade of magenta. When weather is so oppressive, an inferno in the afternoons, and heavy dense air at night and early mornings, you do anything you can to keep your spirits up.

Two weeks ago when we were leaving Fort Lowell pool, Bill recognized Gene arriving and stopped the truck so we could say hi to him.

We had first met Gene his first summer in Tucson 3 years ago. He was driving his friend Natalie's sports car convertible then. Gene had not moved to Tucson yet. He was from New York City and staying with his friend Natalie.

We saw Gene at public pool a second time, and when autumn arrived and public pool prices went thru the roof, and we joined the Club, fairly soon afterwards we discovered Gene and Natalie at the Club.

And I began to schmooze with Gene a lot in the Jacuzzi. He wasn't really a swimmer. Bill became friends with him first and told me Gene is a cartoonist. Gene had lived in his loft in Chelsea in lower Manhattan for 35 years until the landlord figured out how to get it away from him.

Gene said he was born in the South but went to college in Miami, where he met all the New Yorkers, and knew New York was the place for him. And he had lived there his whole life before Natalie invited him to Tucson.

I don't know why he came, maybe originally just for a change. Also his stuff was in storage, altho he has been with Joel for 35 years, he could have lived with Joel. We did see Joel a few times, both at public pool and at club, because Joel is a swimmer. He is same as me, he loves to swim and he swims for long time. And I bet it was because of the joy of swimming outside in winter that Joel agreed to buy the house in Tucson. Gene (like me) has no money but Joel has very good job in New York City.

I don't remember when it was that I heard from Katy, Gene is making his decision now, whether to stay in Tucson, move here (bring his stuff from New York City) or go back. I knew Gene would stay. Even tho Gene was every inch a New Yorker, as I had been when I moved here, and even tho Gene had no intention of moving to Tucson when he arrived, I knew what was conscious for me was below consciousness for Gene.

That he loved Tucson and New York City was over. Then we stopped seeing Gene at the club. Bill was the one who noticed it, "we haven't seen Gene in long time" he said. But I had heard from Natalie he and Joel bought a house. So I figured that fixing up the house was occupying all his energy.

Finally last year we saw Gene at public pool for first time after very long time. He told us all about the house. He had really lucked out. The son of a prominent Tucson businessman had bought a dream house up in the foothills when he got married. But the marriage didn't work out, she moved to Oregon, and he sold the house at a bargain price to Joel and Gene.

They have a whole acre and most beautiful house in world, and views so great they can see Benson off in the distance. It is in the country, up in the hills. When we saw Gene 2 weeks ago he said "it is just me and the bobcats and the rattlesnakes."

Bill told me that night "What a change for a boy from Chelsea to be up there with bobcats and rattlesnakes!"

We had seen him at end of last summer and he said he had landscaped all of it, put in a million plants, and miraculously saved all of them even tho we had heat between 113 and 120 all month of July.

I knew Gene was genius landscaper because when he lived with Natalie he had planted 100 rose bushes for her. Plus he had gotten chickens and they had fresh eggs every day and gave eggs to their neighbors. There is really nothing Gene can't do.

When we saw Gene at public pool last year he said he is very lonely. I knew all about that 3 year turning point.

I said "this is when your friends from New York City stop calling and every time you call them they are busy."

"Yes" Gene said "yes."

And before he has made new friends in Tucson.

"All I can suggest Gene is watch old movies, that is what I did, day and night."

When I saw him two weeks ago, he said it has gotten even lonelier, now Nat won't speak to him, and Joel has not come out for a whole year. I forgot about that. When your New York City friends stop calling and each time you call them they are busy, you still have your first friends in Tucson. Then they all move away or break up with you. That is what is happening to Gene now, his first friends in Tucson are moving away, and his closest friend Natalie won't speak to him.

But I looked at Gene's face and he is a transformed person. His eyes are completely clear, his face is completely clear, he is perfectly beautiful. Like me, he was a mess when he first arrived from New York City. It is a long purification process Gene is going thru. If he can make it thru the boredom and the loneliness he will be new man. He is already a new man. And when that is completed he will find friends in Tucson naturally. It all happens naturally. He needs this time now, altho he doesn't realize it.

The solution which emerged for me was to get interested in the news, and go on internet. But that solution won't work for Gene because it is what he did before he left New York City. That was his New York City life, that, and schmoozing with his friends on the telephone all the time.

My life in NYC was being a writer and schmoozing on the phone all the time. So Gene and I exchanged places. I became interested in news and got on internet. And Gene has become a writer. "I have already written 465 pages" Gene said. I think it is wonderful Gene found writing.

It's funny because when I was in the exact same place Gene is, my NYC friends had stopped calling, my Tucson friends either broke up with me or moved away, I did meet a girl at Udall pool. We chit-chatted in the lane as we swam back and forth. And I knew she was a perfect friend for me. We talked about books, and she said "*Angela's Ashes,* that was great," and assumed I had read it.

I had heard of it, so I said "it is great." I finally did read *Angela's Ashes* last week and it is great, just as great as she said it was.

And I knew I could have made a move to make her my friend then. It was before I was on internet or email but I could have offered to exchange phone numbers, or made some move. But I let her slip thru my fingers.

That is when I realized I wasn't ready for friends yet. That secretly I liked this big space in my life without friends. And I think that is what Gene is going thru now. Because when I told him about the writers meeting at Barnes & Noble for free on 3rd Wednesday of every month, he really wasn't interested.

And last summer when he was so desperately lonely I reminded him everyone at the club loves him, but he said he doesn't have the money.

Bill enjoys Gene's friendship and always hopes Gene will be at the pool so he can have someone to talk to, but Gene never shows up. And I noticed in the parking lot two weeks ago, as overjoyed as Gene was to see us, it didn't occur to him, when I said "I have gone back to my writing," to say "let's exchange emails and send each other our new writing."

He let me and Bill slip thru his fingers, just as I had done with the wonderful woman I met at Udall pool, even tho I knew she was the perfect new friend for me

Under the desk with Ruthie

Ruthie made a glorious video and put it on internet so all could see it.

Two years ago she gave a little class in palmistry, and she asked her friend to video it so she could see herself as a teacher. And she found the video so interesting, that when she began to put photos up on her web page, she realized she would be able to put up her video, that she could share it.

So last week I got the email with the link and then phone call from Ruthie saying "watch it Anne." But I had no idea where the speakers for my computer were. They used to be on my desk, but now they were no longer on my desk. I assumed I must have put them away somewhere. And I said "tomorrow I will look for them," and Ruthie said "press the link to the video, at least you will be able to see me."

But when I pressed the link nothing showed. Ruthie called again the next day, and when nothing showed again the next day, something came on saying if I download adobe flash reader I will be able to see it. So I downloaded it, but again nothing showed. So I assumed I had computer problems, and Ruthie was heart broken.

But the next day I pressed Ruthie's link again, and this time the whole video showed, but there was no sound, but it was thrilling for me to see my friend Ruthie. That was exciting. I looked all over for my speakers, and eventually I found them, they had fallen off behind my desk, and the wires seemed to be still plugged in. Because when I pressed the "on" button, a green light went on, showing me it was on, but no matter what I did I could not get sound.

When Ruthie called I told her I loved the video picture but I could not get sound. And she had me try to play a song to see if sound worked for anything. And when the song didn't play, she said "the problem is your speakers, Walmart sells them for 30 dollars, you need new speakers."

Then I got email from her saying she will send me the 30 dollars so I can buy new speakers. Then in the evening while Bill was watching our team, the Arizona Wildcats, play Steve Austin in our stadium in Tucson, a big and very important game, Ruthie called and said "I am writing out the check now, what is your house address?"

But before I gave her my house address, we discussed my speakers. I told her how the green light is on so it is connected, and I assume when they fell down in back of desk for whole year that dust and dog hair etc must have gotten into them and ruined them.

Ruthie said "maybe it is attached to wrong outlet in your computer, maybe you have it attached to microphone."

I said "but I listened to something last year, and no one has changed the connection since then, Bill had connected them for me then."

Ruthie said the green light going on when I press "on" simply means the speakers are attached to electricity, that electricity is flowing into them, it doesn't mean it is attached to the computer, and why don't I look.

I said "but it is dark now Ruthie, and my desk light is so small, I can't see anything."

And she said "do you have a flashlight?" and I said "yes we do."

So I said "Bill is the technician, I don't know how to do anything, I will ask him to come in during the commercial of the football game and see if the wire from the speaker is attached to the computer in the right place."

So I went in and asked Bill. And he said "it is too dark, he will do it next morning."

And I said "what about with a flashlight?"

And he said "I don't want to crawl under your desk with a flashlight now, I am watching the game, I will do it next morning."

So Ruthie said "why don't you do it then, Anne."

So I asked Bill "where is the flashlight?"

And he turned it on for me because flashlights are no longer the same as when I was little girl.

And he got the flashlight and turned it on for me, and he said "I don't know why you want to do it now, it is so messy behind your desk, it is dark, there are so many cords there, you will break your computer and it is not my fault."

I told Ruthie what he said but neither of us were daunted by it. Once I had a problem with something and called the technician, I no longer remember what it was. The technician was a woman. And at first when she told me what to do, I said "wait let me get my husband, he is the technician, I don't know how to do anything."

But either Bill was not available or I had a brainstorm. I

changed my mind. I said "maybe I can do it, I am so used to thinking he can do everything and I can't do anything, but maybe I can do it, you tell me what to do."

And she said, "There you go! you can do it! I'll help you, you can do it." She had so much confidence in me that I got confidence and I followed her instructions and I did it.

And I remembered that when Ruthie said "why don't you do it Anne." And I got so excited, everyone likes a challenge, a project; it is fun and exciting, an adventure.

I reported to Ruthie "there are 3 wires going out of my speaker."

And she said "one goes to the computer, that is the one we have to find."

I crawled under my desk and saw the 3 wires coming from it, and saw that one went into the little hole in back of computer cabinet leading to computer.

Then Ruthie tried to explain to me the right place in computer where it should be. And I said "wait, the first thing is for me to find that small white cord, because when I took the computer out, there was no small white cord attached to it."

I took the little flashlight and sure enough there was a little white cord just dangling, not attached to anything.

Eureka! Maybe that explained why I wasn't getting any sound. So then Ruthie tried to explain the place it should go in.

And there were the 3 little holes next to each other at the bottom with 3 different colors next to them. And Ruthie said "we will just try all of them, and see which one works."

So I plugged it into the middle one.

And Ruthie said "see if the song I sent you on email comes on."

And we both looked on our computers to try to find that email so we could find the link to the song.

And Ruthie said "here it is, scroll up in your email," and she gave me the date and topic. So I clicked on the link to the song, and "Music Match" came on. I had downloaded "Music Match" when Ruthie had tried to see if I got any sound when I did the song.

And then instantly the song began to play. I heard it, it had "happy birthday" in it. Ruthie heard it too.

"Great!" she said, "now x out of it."

I was going to look for the email where she sent me link to her video, but I remembered I had saved it on "favorites," it had been so much fun to see Ruthie and I wanted to show Bill.

So I clicked on "favorites" and there it was. And I clicked it on, and instantly there was Ruthie, I could see her and there was Ruthie talking I could hear her, it was so exciting.

And then we both got very quiet and listened to Ruthie and watched her on our computers while I was on the phone. It was much better than watching Ruthie with no sound. With no sound, even tho it was thrilling to see Ruthie, because there was no content to what she was doing, all I did was make observations like "maybe Ruthie should be wearing lipstick."

Her voice was lovely, and every word she said was fascinating. I loved the video and I learned so much.

My Yesterday

There is an atmosphere of Spring. Maybe because I have my window open and can hear the birds talking to each other. I had the windows shut and the heat on for the whole past freezing nights month. But the heat bill arrived yesterday and I fainted.

So last night I did different regime. Bill shut the windows and turned on the space heater in his room and watched a big football game. I went to my backroom with window wide open, burrowed under 4 comforters and flannel sheet, and watched tv till I dropped off to sleep.

And when I woke up I made the coffee and opened up all the windows and doors. I never used to open the windows and doors when I first woke up, because the heat was still on and I didn't want to let it out. And I wanted to leave the heat on till Bill woke up, so he would wake up to toasty house. But luxury of waking up to toasty house went out the window when I saw heating bill for $345.

So this morning I put on 3 flannel shirts over my long sleeved top, and came in and opened up both windows in my computer room, I could let the air in because there was no heat to let out.

And the result is the atmosphere of the morning came in the open window with the air. I heard all the birds chirping, I have not woken up to the sound of birds chirping for past 6 weeks, the whole era of heat in the house. It is a nice sound to wake up to. That bird chirping has such a steady sound to it, I wonder if the birds are nest building.

I had big heavy dreams last night. The era we are now in is interesting because no day is in any way like the day before. Last night I dozed off just when "Matlock" was beginning. I had waited up to 11 to see it. And then slept all thru the night till 7:30. But the night before I was up very late and then woke up totally wide awake at 4 am. Each night's sleep pattern is opposite to night before, and I have a hunch the rhythm of the days will not be one bit like matched pearls on a string, but each be totally unique.

The blue sky has some white streaks of clouds. There is

atmosphere of earliest day of Spring with damp breezes. But Spring swings both ways, it comes on the sound of the birds when the air is perfectly dry and warm and first balminess has entered. But it also comes with hint of damp chill in blue sky, because it brings the awareness winter is moderating itself, it feels like the transition from winter to spring.

When I woke up yesterday I wondered if another cosmic energy packet had arrived. I was totally wide awake at 4 am, as if a huge jolt arrived, a very wide awake energy, and it wasn't any energy I could work with yet. It was like raw energy. I didn't know what to do with myself. So I posted on a news forum. It was pitch black outside. And I stayed on my forum till it was warm enough to sunbathe in sunshine on outside couch in backyard. That was when I fully noticed how odds and ends I was.

And when I realized new energy had arrived, because the symptoms were familiar. Even tho I had that upset tummy which goes with new energy, I wanted to eat in a restaurant, and have different food than I have at home, and have it be prepared by someone else. And then I wanted to go to the mall and look at the clothes on sale and buy something. I wanted an adventure, to be totally away from my regular routine, and I wanted big treats of all kinds.

I wanted to be taken out to a restaurant for a tuna fish sandwich, I wanted to go to a store where the clothes were 80 per cent off. I didn't want my homebody routine with just a swim to refresh the day. I wanted a whole big day totally out of my routine.

When Bill got back from walking Beanie I informed him of my ideas. And he didn't go for any of them. But finally he said he would be willing to take me to the restaurant before my swim. I was so excited. I really really really wanted to go to a restaurant.

Restaurants have completely dropped out of my life because Bill doesn't like going to them. The more freedom we give each other, the more apparent it becomes that some things we just like differently. I love restaurants, he doesn't. I like to eat in the middle of the day, he likes to eat at 11 pm. We each used to force ourselves to accommodate the other, but it is working out much happier now that we each let the other go their own way.

He took me to Alice's for my lunch, which turned out to be smart move. Because instead of forcing himself to sit there and order and eat when he didn't want to, he went to

St Vincent's next door and looked at their used books. They had sale of 5 books for a dollar.

And when waitress told me their special is mushroom cheeseburger, it is a great price, I said "I want a tuna fish sandwich."

She said "if you have taste for tuna fish sandwich that is what you want, and we make it good here, also our chicken salad sandwiches are to die for."

I forgot I loved chicken salad sandwiches and switched my order. It was 50 cents more if you order it on a French roll, but I thought then maybe it will be bigger sandwich. So I did. And for the side I chose French fries. And the sandwich came with lettuce and tomato on it.

And I tell you there was no happier girl than me, eating her delicious chicken salad sandwich on French roll with delicious French fries on the side. I enjoyed it so much that for whole rest of day I remembered how much I loved it, and my idea of ideal life was to be taken each afternoon for the very same meal.

I never wanted it to end. We were on the clock because Jerry's pool closes at 2:30 and we had arrived at restaurant at 1:10. So while I was waiting for my order to be brought to me, I asked her if it was ok if I went next door to the bakery.

We had stopped at the bakery on Saturday. And I had gotten a loaf of bread, some hamburger rolls, 2 sticky buns, and I told her I wanted that small chocolate cake, but she hadn't heard me about the chocolate cake. I realized when we were on way to pool afterwards that the price was too low to have included the cake and there was no cake.

But my mind was totally taken up with what she had told me about her beloved dog Charley. She had Charley since she was baby puppy, she has another dog too. And vet had just charged $600 to tell her he would have to operate and do a test and Charley is 13, she might not live thru the operation. And the woman in the bakery was so upset and didn't know what to do.

So of course I asked my Higher Self, who said, "don't bring Charley back to the vet, Charley is fine, don't bring her for the 1200 dollar operation, and she doesn't need the test, she is fine."

All I said to the woman at the time was "I will pray for Charley with all my heart." But when I got in the car with Bill I told him all the details. And he asked his Higher Self and got the same answer I did. That "Charley is fine, and no more vet visits, let her heal herself."

So you can see why yesterday, when I was next door to the bakery ordering my lunch, I wanted to use the time to go to the bakery, and get the chocolate cake which had been forgotten, and to tell my friend exactly what my Higher Self told me. It is so hard for people who are not tuned into their Higher Self because their vet tells them one thing, and they really don't know what to do.

And the vet had not even been decisive, he said "she may not make it thru the operation." And I hope I am wrong about this, but the idea had come up at vet's office about putting her dog to sleep.

I had the wits before I left on Saturday to at least say "no operation" and "Charley will live another 5 years." Which is what my Higher Self said.

But when I went in yesterday and she was there, I was very explicit. I didn't say "I talked to my Higher Self" because I don't know if people understand what that means.

But I said "I prayed to God and this is what I was told." And then I said about not bringing Charley back to vet, no operation, and that Charley is fine, and she will heal herself; and just to give her all the treats she likes because high spirits heal anything.

And I said "my husband also prayed to God and got the same answer I did." And you could see her eyes light up with joy and hope. No one but me had told her any good news, and that was a girl who wanted more than anything else in the world to hear good news about her dog.

And even tho my lunch was the most delicious lunch in the world, at a certain point I did speed up, because the clock was right in front of me, and I wanted to have time to get Bill at St Vincent's and bring him into the bakery, so he could tell the woman the same thing I did. We had both agreed in the car that our Higher Self gave us the identical information.

So I asked waitress for to-go carton, and put second half of sandwich in that and rest of the yummy French fries, and found Bill in St Vincent's. I hadn't known about the 5 books for a dollar sale. Bill was ecstatic and chose 5 books. And I said "come to the bakery and tell the lady what your Higher Self said about her dog, her dog is named Charley, I already told her what my Higher Self said." And Bill said "OK."

So I brought him and introduced her, and she said to him "you heard the same thing?"

And he began to tell the story about our dog. And I went

to the car with the chocolate cake and the to-go carton with 2nd half of my lunch, and we drove to the pool. We'd still have half hour to swim.

Bill was ecstatic about the books, I was ecstatic about my lunch, but both of our hearts were really with the woman in the bakery. But I felt we had done as much as we could do to help her. And when I talked to my Higher Self in the car she promised Charley would be fine, that we had made exactly the right suggestions to the woman in the bakery.

We arrived for last half hour of swim and parking lot was jammed, and I knew pool would be jammed with all the new businessmen, but I didn't care.

I was no longer at loose ends like in the morning, everything had coalesced for me. I had my delicious lunch, and all weekend I had wanted to go back and reassure the woman in the bakery. And I was united with Bill which always makes me happy.

We had been at odds with each other when we first got in car to set off. But now we were perfectly joined. We were joined because we each had had perfect satisfaction in our outing, and we were joined because we both wanted to help the woman in the bakery with all our hearts. And whether or not she chose to listen to our suggestions, we knew we had brought her the wisdom of Heaven to bear on her problem, and that is a gift.

The swim pool was jammed but I didn't care. Bill's friend Alfredo was just leaving, and it was so nice to see him, we hadn't seen him in a whole year, he is so warm and wonderful and friendly and nice. And Bill arrived with his new friend Doug, who is such a nice guy. Talking about health food is not my favorite topic, but Bill loves to talk about health food with Doug, and then they talk about UFOs on Art Bell's show too.

And we each had a very nice half hour swim. And in the shower I got to talk to that nice woman who works for the school system, she was on her lunch hour, and we had a great time talking to each other.

And when I was leaving Jill was there, and I was so happy to see her and she was so happy to see me. And I brought her out to see Bill, they are friends, so Bill could tell her all about our new dog Beanie, she is animal lover.

Bill was talking to his health food friend, Doug. And Bill told Jill about Beanie (the Humane Society had him on clearance because no one would adopt him). And Jill told Bill about the greyhound she had adopted from Greyhound

Rescue which no one would adopt.

And Jill had asked me, before we arrived at Bill and Doug, "have you fallen in love with Beanie?"

And I said "yes we have."

And she said "it's amazing how fast it happens."

And I said "yes."

She said "they don't replace the old dog, no one can, but you fall in love with them anyway."

And I said "yes, that is just what happened."

And Jill is exactly right. I don't know what it is about Beanie, but it is irresistible, he is irresistible, Bill and I have both fallen in love with him. And even tho Lulu acts like she can't stand him, my Higher Self said Lulu loves him too.

They gossip about me on forum

Nothing in the whole wide world is as gossipy as a libertarian news forum. There have been long endless gossipy threads discussing everyone who has ever been on these forums. And there have been a few gossipy threads about me too in the past.

These threads are made up of posts which attack you, posts which defend you, and then posts which discuss you ad infinitum.

I never read any of the threads about me in the past, I thought I'd get my feelings hurt. And I was extremely surprised I read this one on a spin-off forum yesterday.

This forum is much smaller, there are not so many posters, and not so many there know me, so it was a short thread.

And to my amazement I was detached and fascinated. I

just found it so interesting I was a topic under discussion.

(Palo is my screen-name on the forum)

One said I was the stupidest person on god's green earth.

And another one said "Palo is not as stupid as she seems."

And another one said "Palo has changed, recently she is not as stupid as she used to be."

One said "if Palo has left her old forum she is welcomed here."

And another said "she has a lot of apologies to make before she is welcomed here."

One said "Palo is so stupid, she must be a secret government agent, posting to throw us off the track."

Another said "no, she's not a secret government agent posting to throw us off the track, she is a hippy from the '60s who never grew up."

And then they lost interest talking about me and began to argue among themselves about the President.

Steve's Great Writers Meeting Last Night

Last night was the writers meeting at Barnes & Noble on how to get published. There hasn't been one in months. There was supposed to be one last month, and I showed up, but it turned out to be false alarm, no one showed up but me.

This time Steve the facilitator was already there when I arrived and so were two other women. By the time the meeting started there were two more women and one man, and when I looked up there was Sophia. And by the time we finished introducing ourselves, saying our name and what we write, there was actually a whole crowd of people, mostly men, who had brought up chairs and were sitting behind Steve.

By then Steve had launched into his spiel, so we never

got to hear their names and what they write, which is too bad. I was sitting next to Steve at the table and when he took a breath in his spiel I told him there were so many sitting behind him.

It was my hint he might want to ask them to introduce themselves too. But instead he said "I am surrounded" and went back to his spiel. They all left before the meeting broke up so I never got to meet them or hear anything about them, which is too bad since I like hearing what people write.

The woman next to me writes short stories, but none of them are related to each other. When Steve suggested she turn them into a novel, "a novel is just a whole bunch of stories" Steve said, she said "I don't know how to do it, because they are not related to each other in any way." I think her name is Carol. I liked her.

Across from Carol was Emily. Emily said she had been writing a memoir but then a friend of hers committed suicide because he was scared to death. She said it began as a family fight over money and what scared him to death turned out to be a hoax but he didn't know that. By that time he was no longer in the world. Emily said she had been a drug counselor and also addicted to drugs herself and her memoir had been about her experiences as a drug counselor, but now she was writing this book instead.

Her big concern is that because it is about someone else's life not hers, about getting the details right. She said instead of calling it "a true story" she is now going to call it "based on a true story" or "inspired by" then she doesn't have to worry about being perfectly accurate. Also she said she is so one-sided about it, she is on his side, that she offered a famous author to help her write it, so it would take in both sides. I don't know if she has heard back from the famous author.

An attractive woman had quizzed Steve before she introduced herself.

"Let's hear about you" she said, "what have you published? Have you been published by a real place or just vanity press?"

Steve said the book he has had published is about his own flying experiences and it was published by a subdivision of Random House.

"O" she said, "I got the impression from the flyer you were just published by a vanity press." She said she has not started to write yet, but she wants to.

The woman next to her said she is a poet and also an

artist and a few other things. She has those dismal looks of a poet in a comic book. Thin, bedraggled, long hair which did not look attractive, and an unhappy mien. She was not a walking advertisement for her poetry. She looked like someone who could be cast in a play as an unhappy poet writing unhappy poetry. She is definitely someone who needs to spruce herself up a bit, put her hair up, put on a little lipstick, smile, and wear a pretty dress. And a little jewelry to bring herself some sparkle.

Sophia is a beautician and of course she looked beautiful as always. When Steve talked about the new book he is writing about a menage-a-trois, he said the devastating femme fatale looks just like Sophia. Sophia perked up. Steve really wanted to write his second book about a particular airplane he is in love with, but all his friends told him "O no! not another airplane book! we want to read about people."

So instead Steve is writing about this menage-a-trois where "the man is totally insensitive to women, sees them as just another notch on his belt," according to Steve, and the devastating femme fatale looks just like Sophia.

Personally I think Steve should write the book about the airplane he is in love with instead of about these people he doesn't like. But Steve is finding it such an intriguing challenge to write this book, so why not.

He said he began it as a romance novel, there is huge market for romance novels. He said the audience for romance novels is girls between the age of 15 and 17, because after 17 they start to have their own experiences and prefer that to reading about the experiences of others. He was told to put in 3 explicit sex scenes, he wrote two and has to write another. He finds them very hard to write.

Between you and me, I think it would be a more interesting book if Steve wrote his experiences trying to write this book. It all just sounds so far out to me. Here is Steve working for Hughes Aircraft, trying to write a romance novel which exactly meets the criteria of romance novels for 15 year olds.

There was also a man at our table. He said he kept a journal when he lived in a Far Eastern country, I forget which country it was now, it is one of those names which are obscure to me, and he would like to turn the journal into a book. He looked like a nice man and I bet his experiences were interesting.

A lot of the advice Steve gave on how to get published is not very usable for me. For instance Steve said he got sick and tired of writing query letters to publishers, and he realized if you take over a wheelbarrow of money you can get someone to do all that for you. They will write the query letters, they will find you an agent, they will edit your book, etc etc.

Apparently there are a lot of people in Tucson who will do everything for you to get published if you just bring over a wheelbarrow of money. Altho who knows, maybe I will win the lottery, and I can do what Steve is doing. Take over the book I wrote back in NYC and wheelbarrow of money, and dump it all in someone else's lap, for a small fortune they will do it all for me.

Steve did say something which really made me perk up tho. He said the Southwest Authors Society has a workshop for two days once a year, where agents arrive from all over the country and critique your work. I don't know how much it costs, all of Steve's suggestions involve money. He said he watched thru the door while his friend DR was having her work critiqued by the agent. He said "DR had her head in her hands the whole time so I thought it was bad news" but instead the agent took both of DR's books, he bought them on the spot.

This meant a lot to me, because at my second meeting at

Barnes & Noble Steve was absent, and he had sent DR to fill in for him. She told us how she got her first book published but how she cannot get her two new books published for love or money. Each time she sends them out they come right back. She said "one just came back this morning but she has to buck up and send it right back out again, but it is wearing her down."

I totally identified with her experience of how it is wearing her down. I had been in that boat and I had given up. I had decided it was all futile. But here a year later, Steve reports that by going to the Southwest Authors workshop a literary agent bought both her books.

I would gladly save my pennies for the $250 for the workshop if I thought it would work out that way for me too. In fact I would be willing to complete a second manuscript by the time the next workshop rolls around in September. Why can't lightning strike twice, for DR and for Anne.

Steve also said small presses have come into their own during the past recent years. This is news to me. All my experience with trying to get published comes from my years living in NYC. 14 years have now gone by and I am beginning to understand huge changes have taken place in publishing world. What I learned from my experience back then no longer applies, there have been developments. Steve made it very clear big publishing houses don't want books, except for how-to books, or mysteries, or romance, but small presses do want books.

A man who was just traveling thru Tucson, he had arrived to help his mom, she is having operation, he travels around in his RV and has just come back from fishing in Mexico, said "Anne, there are small presses in Tucson, why don't you just go down there and talk to the people."

He also said "the key thing is just to have something out there published in any way, after that you can talk to people because you have something published." He said "even if you publish it yourself, it makes no difference, at least it is out there."

He also told me that my manuscript from New York City which I had put on the big floppy discs which everyone used back then, I don't have to retype for smaller disc, there is a place in Tucson which transfers the disc for you. This was an answer to a prayer. As for the whole past year I was wondering how I was going to force myself to face retyping all those New York City stories again.

I don't know who that man is, I don't remember his

name, but he was an angel who showed up at our writers meeting in Barnes & Noble last night, who had a lot of solutions for me.

When the meeting was over the woman next to me, the one who is also a short story writer, said "would it embarrass you Steve if we applauded." We all did. It was a great meeting. And she said "O Steve you are blushing."

Room service at Dracula's castle

It rained during the night. There are puddles in the yard and everything is damp.

We got to the writers meeting at Barnes & Noble early last evening and I was surprised it had already started. A woman named Emily, who had been at a previous meeting, was there. And a man and woman I didn't know. It turns out she is the wife of the man. Because mid-meeting I turned to her and said "what do you write?"

And she said "I don't write anything, I am his wife."

I said "well being a wife is harder than being a writer."

And to my surprise everyone at the table turned to me as if that was an unusual thing to say.

I said "sure, writing is just one hour in the morning, you make yourself laugh or tell a story, but being a wife means having to keep your mouth shut, and other things too."

Emily said "O like 'stifle yourself Edith.'"

I said "yes."

And she said "is your husband like Archie Bunker?"

I said "no, my husband is a man."

I didn't want to elaborate because I saw Bill just a few feet in front of us at the section of "Fantasy and Science Fiction." He is enjoying the *Hobbit* books so much, he wanted to see what else is written in that genre.

And on the way home he said "they have *Dracula* there, it is only $6.95."

I said "get it, that is the price of dinner in the restaurant, we can afford that."

And when we had supper very late at night (when house turned quiet after the big thunderstorm) Bill told me the start of *Dracula* which he had read while I was at my meeting.

Apparently a man in Transylvania goes to a castle and when he arrives there is no one there. However he is expected, because a nice plate of paprika chicken is prepared for him with a nice vegetable side.

That is as far as he got in telling me the story. Because all of a sudden I remembered that this morning, when I was on the web looking up Alice's address (to send her birthday card) I thought "why don't I look up Mike's address too."

Back in the days when I was first living with Bill our best friends were Cora and Mike. Bill was working days and going to school at nights. And Cora and Mike arrived every evening and I'd sit at kitchen table with them while Bill was at the big desk in other room studying. Cora was a modern dancer and Mike was a modern artist, and that's actually how I became a writer. Bill said "why don't you write."

Bill, Mike, and I had all met at the Paradox, a macrobiotic restaurant on 7th Street in East Village, Manhattan. Bill was working there, and Mike and I used to eat there, and it was a hang-out place. Mike and I spent long evenings there at the long tables in the backyard garden. He was in love with Dino, one of the young men who always hung out there.

But Mike was always upset at him, and when he got very upset he would say "I am going to call immigration and inform them Dino does not have a green card." I think Dino was from Greece. Which is what eventually happened to Dino. Someone did get very very upset with him and informed immigration on him and he was sent back to Greece, but it wasn't Mike who did it, maybe it was one of his other boyfriends.

And then out of the blue yesterday morning, when I googled Alice's address, I typed in "Michael Zebrenski New York City," and there was only one listing, and it was way out in Queens.

'Queens!' I thought, 'Mike has never even been in Queens, can that be right?'

But before Bill started to tell me about "Dracula," he had said his friend Dave is Polish but not Catholic, and I said "I don't think Jan is Catholic either," and talking about our friends who are Polish made me remember Mike.

So even tho I was very interested hearing about the man who arrived at Dracula's castle and no one was there but he was expected and the paprika chicken was prepared for him and the sides, and as Bill started to wax eloquent about what the sides would be, my mind went back to Mike.

I said "I tried to call Mike Zebrenski today." He ignored my interruption, the way he always does when he is in the middle of telling me something which interests him and he wants to finish his thoughts.

I like hearing Bill's stories, half the time when he describes a book to me, Bill's telling of it is more interesting than the book itself. I like the way his mind meanders around certain details, and then he supplies the details he imagines should be there.

None of my interruptions ever interest him in the slightest, but this one did. And after he finished saying what sides he thought it would be, he said "you were saying about Mike Zebrenski?"

And I told him, "do you think Mike is living in Queens now?"

"Could be," he said. And we went over my research on Google and what the man on answering machine sounded like.

Back to the Meeting

Steve wore an orange Hawaiian shirt, a faded orange. The seat to the right of Steve was empty so I took it. The woman's husband took the seat at opposite end of table facing Steve. The wife sat next to her husband. And Emily sat next to the man, who was her friend. Steve seemed relaxed and happy. He greeted me nicely when I arrived and I shyly returned his warm greeting.

The man did most of the talking, he had written many books but there was a hiatus when he didn't write at all and he told us what got him back into writing. His books are at Lulu.com (I do not know what that is), and he makes a little money from that, dribs and drabs, and he would like to make a lot of money from his books.

His questions were about how to get published by mainstream publisher. His last book was a how-to book and I am not very interested in how-to books. Altho Steve told us the biggest market is for romance, mysteries, and how-to books. All of us at the table agreed we don't like romances. Emily pointed out every book has some mystery, some romance, and I now realize some how-to.

At the end of the meeting when Emily said, "is this an on-going meeting which meets every month?"

Steve explained he sees his role as wagon-master, at each meeting he gives out the same information, how to get started in Tucson, what is happening here, who to connect with, how to start writing, and how to get published.

He expects to have new faces at each meeting, he never intended to have groupies.

Which I just ignored since I like showing up every month. And so does Sophia. The reason she wasn't there is because she is in Poland visiting friends and family.

So Emily said "will you be here next month?"

And Steve told us his wife needs him now, he is going

back to LA, and he is retiring from Raytheon, and Andrew will have to find someone to replace him. As for next month there is a chance he will be here, but he doesn't know.

I'm not sure he wants to live in Los Angeles again, he had said Tucson has now gotten too big. But he has his boat there and his airplane there. "My boat has been in storage for 7 years, I have been paying rent on it, it will be nice to be on the water again."

And he has also been paying rent to keep his airplane in storage. So I guess Steve has been here for 7 years. When you work for Raytheon you can work in Los Angeles or in Tucson. Lisa's husband, Todd, has done both also. In fact he works for Raytheon here in Tucson now just like Steve, and used to work for Raytheon in LA just like Steve.

When Steve said Tucson has gotten too big now and we all have to think about moving to Benson, I said "what about Ajo?"

And his face lit up. "You know I recently visited Ajo" he said.

I wonder if he flew there in one of his airplanes because all he talked about was the runway at the Ajo airport. He loved the runway, it is so huge. Apparently that airport with its huge runway was built that way in WW2 for some reason. And Steve said he met a man in Ajo from Border Patrol and raved about the runway to him, and the man said "does Ajo even have an airport?"

Even tho I have never been to Ajo, it is the place I secretly dream about moving to if I leave Tucson. And I am braced for Ajo jokes. According to everyone in Tucson, Ajo is nowhere, has nothing, and no one lives there. Which is not the exact truth, I looked Ajo up on the web and learned a lot about it. But I can see why it is a place where a border patrol man lives and says "I am surprised, does Ajo even have an airport?"

Steve said the reason he may still be in Tucson when the writers meeting takes place next month, is because he wants to show his oldest daughter Tombstone, she has never been there. "She is 35" Steve told us.

When I was cracking jokes about marriage and Emily said "how long have you been married?" I said "forever."

And Steve turned to me and said "I bet not as long as me."

I stared at him for a minute wondering if that could be true, and he said "46 years."

I said "46?" and he said "yes."

And I said "you have been married longer than me." I was impressed, he is in whole other ballpark than me, it was no contest.

When Steve told us his wife needs him now, he is moving back home, the man whose books are at Lulu.com quipped "your wife is taking you back?"

I think it is quite extraordinary his wife has let him live in Tucson for 7 years but I guess when you are married 46 years there is lots of freedom.

So Steve is going back home. His long sojourn in Tucson is over. I had a sadness. Bill said when we were leaving and I told him, "maybe the new person will have new information and you can gain a lot from the new person."

And I knew that was true, but it never occurred to me Steve would leave. He's such a fixture here. He is at the meeting every month at Barnes & Noble when I show up for it, he is at the Southwest Authors Luncheon at the Plaza Hotel when I show up for that.

He is a bedrock of the writers community here in Tucson. And he is the one who got me back into writing. Whenever I drift away from writing now, I just show up at Steve's next meeting and the next day I am writing.

When Emily had asked "are these meetings on-going"

and Steve said how he expects new people to show up each time because he is wagon master, I said "me and Sophia come to every meeting."

And Emily said "who is Sophia?" and Steve said "a friend."

Andrew had come over when the meeting was underway for 10 minutes, the meeting had started before 7 o'clock, its scheduled time to start. He stood behind Steve's back and massaged Steve's shoulders, and Steve said "whoever you are, if you can cook also I'll marry you."

And Andrew introduced Steve saying, "Whatever there is to know about writing or publishing, if Steve doesn't know it, it's not worth knowing."

And Steve said "you are too kind."

Later in answer to Emily's question, he told us Andrew does community relations for Barnes & Noble, and before that he did community relations for the Air Force base here, he has all the connections to newspapers radio and tv.

It is to Steve's great credit, when he does leave Tucson next month, every person who has come across him here, will miss him very much. I have never met anyone less imposing than Steve, and with so much to offer.

I decide to publish a book

Of course all the dramas in my life now are about my book. It didn't begin till last week-end when I decided I wanted to call Wheatmark to ask them a question. I no longer remember my question, maybe I was going to ask them if we could drive down there to see their books.

But when I googled Wheatmark to find their phone number, what I got was the link to their website. And when I clicked that, there was tremendous information about Wheatmark on it, none of which I knew.

I found out it cost $800, which is about $100 more than I thought it would be. I found out it is print-on-demand. I found out they only give me 5 copies, any more I want I have to order.

But all the work of turning it into a book they do. They do ISBN number, whatever that is, and Library of

Congress, whatever that is. They list it on Amazon which is very nice. They give you a glossy front cover, that is a treat.

And for the back cover they want you to write your teaser, something which will make people want to read your book.

I was very interested in everything I learned about Wheatmark on the web. And before I went into the sunshine on my outside couch to think about it all, I emailed the link to my mom. I thought she would be interested to learn about Wheatmark.

When I had first mentioned to her on email I had made the decision to do it, she had been enthusiastic about the idea, but that was before. Neither her nor me knew anything about Wheatmark, so everything I told her came from my imagination, and of course what I pictured was very different from what was.

I thought my mom would enjoy sharing in this enterprise with me, that I would email her all the steps along the way.

When I first lied in the sunshine and thought about what I learned from reading their site, I was daunted. I thought "is this a good deal?" I had assumed when you self-publish you pay them money, but then you get books galore, as many as you could possibly want. I had no idea after 5 free copies I have to pay same price as anyone else.

But as confused indecisive and daunted as I was, my Higher Self was completely decisive. Each time I thought "I don't know if I want Wheatmark," my Higher Self said "you want Wheatmark."

Each time I thought "maybe I should look into something else," my Higher Self said "we're not going to look into anything else, we are doing Wheatmark."

Altho I could not make up my mind, my Higher Self had made up her mind, "we are doing Wheatmark." And at this time in my life I simply do whatever my Higher Self says to do.

Eventually most of the doubts began to dissipate. I still had no idea why Wheatmark was such a good idea, but I stopped questioning it. Oddly enough, what my mind moved on to was the teaser for the back cover. And my Higher Self's two ideas for my teaser on back cover made me laugh out loud so hard that for first time I thought this enterprise might be fun.

My first idea for back cover when I was still lying on sun couch were not the fun ideas which came to me at table.

I thought I would have to put in a blurb saying why I

was such a good writer. That was what I remembered on backs of other people's books, some famous author would write "this book is wonderful and fun and fresh and funny," or whatever.

So I thought I would just write that. That I would get 4 adjectives from my Higher Self, and write that and credit it to "Anne's editor."

It wasn't till I got up and sat at the sun table and lit a cigarette that I remembered the 3 way conversation I had been in in swim pool a few months after I had given Eileen and Katy a booklet of the stories I had written back in NYC. And the 3 of us treaded water and Katy said to Eileen "her writing is a big nothing," and Eileen said "no it's not, it's genre writing, for a small and limited audience who likes that kind of writing." I had giggled inwardly at the time and put it in a tiny short story I wrote the next morning.

So even tho I had planned to write a praiseworthy blurb about my writing from an imaginary person, I thought, Of course I will use that teeny paragraph where Katy called my writing "a big nothing." It just seemed so funny to me that my teaser on back of book to get people to read my book would have my friend calling my writing a big nothing.

And from that moment on I was into my book, I thought this could be a lot of fun.

Sunday evening my mom emailed, "Don't spend $800 to self publish. You have very little money. Save it for a catastrophe." She said "we in the family enjoy your stories, but do you think people will be enticed to buy your book?"

She thought no one would buy it and I was just throwing 800 in the garbage can. I thought she was saying no one would enjoy my stories. And I lost confidence they would. I lost faith in my writing.

So next morning when I went to my machine to work on my book I had lost heart for it. I sat there in emptiness till Bill came back from bringing the car to the mechanic and wasn't exactly sure what he was going to do next.

And then a miracle happened. When I had found the phone number for Wheatmark on Saturday I had actually called and left a message saying "I want to publish my book with Wheatmark, I have some questions to ask." And just when Bill returned from mechanic, the guy from Wheatmark called.

My Higher Self said "tell him you want to look at the books, that you want to come down and see them, that you have decided you want to publish your book with

Wheatmark."

The man's name was Gavin and because of the depression I had been in, the release from it was euphoria. It turned out he had lived in the East Village for 7 years before he left NYC in 2002. He had lived on 9th Street between First and Second. He asked where I had lived. And we each said to each other "I know your block." Then he had moved to Rivington Street. And I said "girl at pool said Delancy Street is now fancy-shmancy, I can't believe it, it used to be a slum."

And he said "it has all changed since you lived there Anne, it is now expensive."

I said "where do regular people live now?"

And he said "far out in Queens."

I said "you mean Flushing, like where I grew up?"

He said Katz's used to be his favorite restaurant. And I said "the 2nd Avenue Deli closed." And he was shocked. He said "I never heard that from my friends back in the East Village." And I said "I didn't either, but the article about it was posted on my news forum."

I said "I practically fell over because who would imagine learning that on a news forum where most of the posters live in Texas, that an article about the 2nd Avenue Deli would go up."

The reason I was so excited and enthusiastic and even a bit wild in my conversation with Gavin, was because his first words to me were so encouraging that I confided about my mother's email to him and its effect on me.

It made him 100 per cent on my side right from the get-go. If my mother was going to discourage me from doing the book, then Gavin was going to encourage me, and he set about making every single word in his phone call and later on when we met, completely encouraging. And he succeeded to the skies. He was an angel when I needed an angel.

We had a long talk about the East Village because Gavin liked talking about it, and I was thrilled that my editor knew the East Village. If he knew Tucson and he knew the East Village then he knew where my stories were coming from. I couldn't believe my luck finding an editor who understood me so well.

It turns out that Gavin isn't my editor. I found out when I arrived there is no editor, no one reads your book. You send it to them on email, they don't even want you to bother printing it up for them on your printer. They print it up from what you send them on email. They format it for you, but no one reads it.

But I didn't know that when I was talking to Gavin, I assumed he was my editor. We had a wonderful conversation, and I thought "O boy, have I lucked out! I found the perfect editor for me."

And I still thought that way during most of the conversation with Gavin in person, when Bill and I went down to Wheatmark. It wasn't till the end of the conversation that I discovered no one reads my book.

Altho by the end of it I think Gavin was curious to read it when it comes out. I told him I wrote a lovely story about the Lower East Side in it and he will like it. He was so clearly more interested in my stories about our old neighborhood than about Tucson.

Altho we both said on phone how much we love Tucson. And he said after he left New York, he lived in Chicago and Washington DC.

And I said "I heard Chicago is wonderful."

And he said "O it is." And he told me all the wonderful things about Chicago.

I said "if I knew how wonderful Chicago was back then, I would have moved there, but now I don't want to live in a big city again, my experience in New York was too relentless, we had no car, we had the dog, we never got out to refresh ourselves in nature." And he said that is what happened to him too.

Our conversation was so wonderful and made me so enthusiastic about doing the book, that when he said "when do you want to come down Anne, why don't you come down now."

My Higher Self said "yes, go for it."

So I said "my husband just got back from car mechanic, he is at loose ends, it is the perfect time for him to drive me, when do you go on your lunch hour?"

He said "it doesn't matter, I will wait for you."

I said "I live at Fifth and Swan."

He said "then it will take you no time to get here."

So my Higher Self said "tell him you will leave in 20 minutes."

So we both said "great!" I was so uninhibited by that time I said "I am just in bulky sweater now from the cold."

He said "it is warming up."

I said "I will put on a bra."

Bill was just starting to eat his lunch, that he had been preparing for himself while I had been on phone with Gavin.

"Will you drive me to Wheatmark?"

He said "OK."

He said "but it's probably way out in the boondocks."

But I looked it up on computer, and they had address and map. And Bill said "it is just two blocks from the swim club, it is not way out in the boondocks, it is close by." He was relieved.

So I found my bra, and a little black blouse with capped sleeves that I had never worn, I forget now which skirt I chose to wear, and black patent leather high heels, where I had cut off the back strap and middle strap yesterday with scissors, because I discovered I never wore them when I had to go to that trouble of strapping them on. I hadn't been able to do a perfect job with scissors so it looked a little trashy.

But the odd thing is, that now that Gavin thought I was an East Villager, I discovered I wanted that East Village trashy look. I hadn't realized how totally suburban my look had become in Tucson, till I put on the patent leather open-toed high heels with scissors marks showing, and realized "perfect! East Village trashy!" Black blouse, black bra, and black skirt completed the look. And I planned to put on red lipstick before I got out of the car (my lipstick was in the car).

And when I got out my new pocketbook, which I like, I thought "O no! this pocketbook is not trashy looking."

I had bought it because it was so pretty, with pinks and purples, but it made me look well-dressed, which is not the East Village trashy look at all. But I didn't have time to look for a pocketbook which might work, and I didn't think I owned any (I have gazillion pocketbooks but none are East Village trashy). And besides I wanted to plan the stuff to put in there so I would have what I needed. I wanted cigs, and a lighter, and a pen. I looked for my new cute notebook to write in but I couldn't find it. And Bill said "take your swimming stuff, we can swim at Jerry's pool afterwards."

So I wrote down the address, and Bill studied the map from Google so he knew just where it was, and we got into the car, and the trip took no time, and he found it right away. And Bill said "I'll sit in the car."

And I said "come in, don't you want to meet my editor."

And he said "OK."

Gavin turned out to be much younger than I pictured. I assumed he was my age, but he looked around 30. He told me he is a writer too, he writes screen plays.

I said "I want my book to be very affordable, I thought

$5.99 would be nice price."

And he brought out a list of what the prices are. And it looked like they would sell my book for $13.99 which seemed a lot to ask people to pay for it.

He said "how long is your book?"

And I said "it will be short, it is just my Tucson stories."

And Bill said "why not put in all your East Village stories too then, make it a bigger book." Bill thought if I was paying $800, put all the stories in the book.

But that wasn't my plan. My Higher Self had come up with a very interesting idea for me. She said "if you are putting all this momentum into publishing a book, keep up the momentum, after you publish this book, keep going, publish your two books of stories you wrote back in NYC." And I planned to do that, even tho it would take big work on my part. Those manuscripts are up in my closet in a manuscript box. But Gavin said if I am willing to pay for it, they can scan them for me.

I told Gavin my East Village stories are hotter than my Tucson stories. For some reason Gavin agreed with me, "just put out the Tucson stories first."

I said "they are not hot, altho there are a few cute ones in there."

Gavin said "what you want Anne is to earn enough from your first book to pay for publishing your second book." And I looked at him with face full of love.

By this time I was totally confused, but Gavin was not, he understood everything. And I told him how I had tortured myself for 2 days after I read how they wanted it formatted, and he said "stop torturing yourself, none of that matters, just send it."

And that was pretty much it. Gavin said he wants to read a copy when it comes out, and he will pay for it.

I said "don't be silly, I'll buy you a copy, you deserve it because you encouraged me."

He told me anyone can order a book from them and get it at the same discount rate I do, 40 per cent off. And a light bulb went off in my head, and I said "I think my mother should pay full price, because she tried to discourage me."

And he said "yes, she has to pay retail."

And I laughed for 5 minutes that my mom has to pay retail.

George

Last evening it hit me I had never written about George. I didn't see how that was possible, but it is. Of course I want to write about George. He was a friend of mine and he was a friend of my dogs.

I am sure anyone who lived in the East Village in the '60s or the '70s or the '80s or the '90s would know George. I don't know when he moved there, and I don't know how long he stayed. In my mind there is no beginning and no end to George. I assume he must have been there forever. Altho of course he was born in Germany (I think) and had thick accent, so I don't know when he came over. If you say to George "how old are you? what country did you come from? where did you go to high school?" If you ask him anything personal, he will not answer.

I know George is Jewish because when we'd be walking down the street with my dog, George helping me do errands, the older men on First Avenue who worked in the stores, would try to pull George into that tiny little synagogue on Houston Street on Friday evenings so they could have a minyon.

Apparently you can't have your service at all unless there is a minyon. I had no idea what a minyon is, I am guessing 6 men with prayer shawls on standing around the rabbi and the cantor, if that synagogue had a cantor at all.

Their eyes would light up when they saw George coming down the street with me and my dog, because it was so close to the time, and they needed that extra person to make a minyon. I have no idea if George acceded to their request or not. I mean when he finished helping me, did he go over to the synagogue? I do not know.

George's claim to fame is that he had been at City Hall thru umpteen administrations. They all knew him at City Hall. When I told that to my fellow dog walkers in Tompkins Square Park, they scoffed!

"He is a meshuginar," they said to me.

"He *thinks* he goes to City Hall every day and they all know him there," they said to me.

They said "it is like the meshuginar who was in the middle of First Avenue waving his arms last week, he thought he was a traffic cop directing traffic, and George thinks he goes to City Hall every day and he is known there."

That is what Mike said.

Mike is a horse-playing Jewish man, exactly the same age as my father. Mike was born in 1913, like my dad and like Bill's dad, and is a horseplayer like Bill's dad, goes to the track every day.

In a competition of the most stubborn man on earth, is it Leon my dad? is it Bill's dad? is it Mike the dog walker in Tompkins Square Park? They are all heavy-weight champions in the area of scoffing— stubborn-minded scoffers. But I guess I would give the award to Mike.

There is nothing I could say or do, which would change Mike's mind that George imagines he goes to City Hall every day, that George is a meshuginar with a vivid imagination.

If Mayor Abe Beame happened to be walking thru Tompkins Square Park (which he would never do!) and came up to George and said "Hi George, how are you doing" and if Mike were sitting next to George, Mike would still not change his mind.

And in fact a year or so before I left New York, George

was at City Hall when Mayor Beame showed up for a luncheon. He had been mayor a few administrations before. "Hi George, you still here?" former Mayor Abe Beame said. And George said "yes, your honor."

I know exactly how George got to be "included" at City Hall because he used the same technique on me and it worked like a charm. Yes it's true the whole world sees George as a meshuginar, but that is before you get to know him. After you get to know him, I am not saying George is not a meshuginar, but who cares!

He just gives you a more expansive view of what human nature is like. Like discovering a new planet in the solar system or new star in the galaxy. Your vision widens to include George. (Before you get to know George, he is not included in your vision, there is the solar system and there is George, and he is excluded.) It is a big difference.

And in some ways now I feel myself privileged to be one of those who knows George. Altho of course everyone thru a zillion administrations knows George, plus half my neighborhood. I am not in small club. Half my neighborhood just knows George as meshuginar and excludes him. And half know him as I do, and everyone at City Hall, and the old men who try to pull him into their minyon.

The way George became my friend, and got to be included in City Hall, is by making himself indispensable. I used to always run away from George. But one day I was coming home with all those heavy shopping bags, plus I had my dog, and George offered to carry my shopping bags. It was help I desperately needed.

And to my surprise my dog, it was my first dog then, Spes, was madly passionately totally in love with George. George not only carried all my shopping bags home for me, but carried them up the 3 flights of steps and put them by my door. It made my life so much easier, it was such a huge favor.

And after that he figured out my habits, that I went to the park every day with the fellow dog walkers, and then grocery shopped on First Avenue on the way home. And it seems just at the instant I was trying to navigate all those heavy bags, George would appear, carry them home and up all the steps. And of course my dog was overjoyed out of her mind to be with George, she loved George.

And then somehow that became our routine. My dog Spes never liked going to the park with the fellow dog-walkers, so instead George and I would walk around the neighborhood with her as I stopped in stores to pick up this or that. Once the 3 of us walked to SoHo together to the discount paper store and I bought 10 heavy packages of top quality typing paper, and George carried it all home for me.

When I got one of those huge Selectric typewriters because they cost nothing when computers came in, and it broke a few times, George carried that huge heavy thing downstairs. And we took taxi together to Chelsea to my typewriter store to have it fixed. And then George and I and dog walked home. Same thing when we picked it up. I do not know how I would have managed without George.

And this is exactly what happened at City Hall. I have no idea where in City Hall the big machers spent all day schmoozing. But it was very convenient for them, if someone wanted container of coffee to-go, with bagel and shmear, that George was always there, eager and willing to go.

Whatever anyone had a taste for, there was George. They only had to give him the money for it and he would go across the street and get it. There were probably lots of errands they could send George for. To get their cigars, to get their cigarettes. If they bought their cigars in a different neighborhood, George would go get it! Anything! wherever it was!

When Isaac Bashevis Singer was invited for tea, it was George who bought the napkins, who bought the cookies, and even poured out the coffee and tea. He told me later "Isaac Bashevis Singer had tea not coffee, just lemon no sugar, and didn't eat any of the cookies." That might have been where former Mayor Abe Beame showed up and said "I see you're still here, George" and George said "nice to see you, your honor."

Even if something was on another floor, they could send George to get it. With George around no one had to move a muscle, George would get it for you. They couldn't run away from George like I did the first ten years, they were stuck with him from the beginning, so I bet they discovered very quickly how indispensable George is. It hit me once that Mayors come and go but George is always there.

I tried to explain this to Mike. But you can get a good idea what my dad was like and Bill's dad was like. All Mike did was to say again about the meshuginar on First Avenue, how he stood there waving his arms directing traffic, till the cops finally took him away. Mike refused to believe George ever stepped foot in City Hall.

The very few personal things I know about George are

things he let drop, because as I say he wouldn't answer any question. One very cold day in winter he mentioned, during the Depression in Germany he would go to the public library because it was the only warm place.

But when I said "did you come from Germany, George?" He gave that odd look and either said "no" or refused to answer.

Once he said his uncle is still mad at him, because he accuses George of stealing the bottle of whiskey at his daughter's bas mitzvah, which of course George did.

"I didn't know you have family here?" I said.

And George refused to answer. That is the only time George mentioned any family at all.

I have the impression George might have gone to high school here and had a terrible time, no one talked to him. But I may not be right about this, it may be some other early experience in America where things were awful for George.

When my dog Spes was ill, George was my savior. He arrived every day, and when she could no longer make the steps, he carried her down, he carried her up, and she would walk with us to the card tables by the precinct across the street, where she would lie under the table while

George and I played cards.

I did this because she wanted to be outside so much. So George and I would spend hours upon hours playing cards. I was absolutely completely devoted to my dog, I would do anything for her, and George was a saint and angel to do this for me.

That's really when George and I became close. He was the worst card player in the world. We played Gin Rummy, and at first I easily beat him every game, even tho I had not played cards since I was 9 years old. But when I saw how much George wanted to win, I managed to lose every game after that.

George kept score with pencil and paper. Sometimes George, who was up every night and never slept, would fold his arms on the table, rest his head on it, and say "wake me up with a kiss." I wish I could replicate George's heavy accent "vake me up mit a kiss." It was hard to understand George cause of his heavy accent.

After two months Spes did go to Heaven, early one Saturday morning. Bill and I spent the whole day at home together talking being close. At 4 pm the intercom bell rang, and I thought to myself "that is George! he is so faithful! he is here to help me walk Spes."

I wasn't ready to say anything, I just buzzed George in and called down the stairs "thank you very much George, but I am already back home."

But that evening when I went out to buy something at the corner store, George passed me on First Avenue. I said "George, Spes went to Heaven this morning, Bill and I are upstairs sitting shiva for her right now."

And a smile crossed George's lips when I said I was sitting shiva for Spes. And he said "I thought if she made it thru the weekend she would be OK."

How sweet of George to have had faith in my dog, that she could make it! I had too, till she went to Heaven. But I tell you, it took all the faith in the Universe for me to have believed that. No one will ever know the effort I put into having faith and hope my dog would make it.

Then Bill took me on camping trip in Adirondacks for 4 or 5 days so we could recuperate from Spes and the day we got back we got Clio. Adina had brought Clio over the day before we left, to ask if we wanted her. She couldn't stand Clio and was giving Clio up. And she came up with Clio, and Bill said "fine we will take her!"

But we were going on camping trip. We asked Adina to keep Clio for those few days. Adina clearly never wanted

Clio back in her apartment but of course she said yes, she was so relieved she had found a home for Clio. And Bill had me call from Grand Central Station when we got off the train, to tell Adina we will take taxi home now and to bring Clio over right now.

Clio was 4 months old and a torture chamber, and she could not be walked off the leash the way I did with Spes. She had to be on the leash every second, because when she wasn't she took off faster than lightning and danced in First Avenue in heavy traffic. That girl gave me so many traumas!

But George and I took up where we left off. I had to hold Clio on the leash, so it would have been even harder to carry home all those shopping bags of groceries. But I didn't need to, I had George. I was very close to George now and loved him beyond measure for what he had done for Spes, my beloved beloved beloved Spes.

And it turned out what George wanted, I don't know how we arrived at this, what George wanted was— after I threw the ball for Clio at the school playground across from the precinct, the girl was a great athlete— We would sit on the bench or at the card table, I would have Clio on the leash. George would bring pencil and paper, and he would dictate a letter.

It began off as one letter, he had something he really wanted to say to someone at City Hall about how things should be. I copied down his dictation in good English with punctuation, and then had George type it up, and I proofread it.

It didn't matter what I wrote down in perfect spelling and good English. By the time George typed it up, the spelling was a catastrophe and there was no punctuation. The first time I had him redo it, but after that I didn't bother. I would read him back his letter after I first took it down, and then read it back to him after he brought me the typewritten copy. George was very satisfied, he liked hearing his letter. George never said "I" in the letter, he didn't say "I think." He always said "we." "We think" "We suggest" "What we think you should do.."

After the first few letters George discovered he loved this so much, that I would sit on the bench with him and take down 10 letters. Since George did not have very much to say, and would only try to think of something to say and to who he could possibly write to, the letters became very brief.

"Perfect!" I would say after I took it down.

"Perfect!" I would say, after he showed me the typewritten letters from the ones I had taken down day before. I thought "what does it matter all the typos and spelling mistakes," some of the letters were so silly, George's suggestion for the type of teabags they use at City Hall. All the letters were to City Hall.

I said to George "I am your secretary," and he loved that. After that wherever we went, which was everywhere in our neighborhood, and whoever we met, and George knew everyone in the neighborhood, he introduced me as his secretary. "This is my secretary" he would say.

And they would look at me (they didn't believe George) "yes" I said, "I am his secretary."

George loved having a secretary. And somehow it is my destiny lol, to always be a secretary. In one way or another, my whole life I have been a secretary. I am one to this day.

Clio was 4 months old when we adopted her, and 4 years old when we moved to Tucson, so this life must have continued till the day we left. He would help me with my shopping while I walked Clio, then we would sit on the bench, and I would be his secretary, and then he would keep me company while I threw the ball for Clio at the handball courts.

Clio loved George too, all dogs loved George.

I didn't tell George I was leaving, I knew it would break his heart. But he found out after we left, and he handled it well. I wrote to all my neighbors and friends in the neighborhood "if you see George give him my address in Tucson, and tell him to write."

And sure enough I got a letter. He must have come to my building to find me and Simone came down and gave him my address. And I got a letter from him saying "now he doesn't have his secretary," but it was still a nice letter—if you could figure out what he was saying, every word was misspelt and it was one long sentence.

("dear secriterti" it began off.) He wouldn't tell me his address, he kept everything about his life secret to the end. I never even know which block he lived on. He told me to write to him at the Democratic headquarters on 9th Street and gave me their address, which is a storefront on 9th Street.

And so George and I corresponded for about a year. And then I guess I forgot about George and he forgot about me. But he has a place in my heart which will always be there. And I bet George too has never forgotten, that one day he had a great secretary.

Post script, I remember now when George and I sat on the bench to be his secretary, first I had George get me a container of coffee to-go, sweet and light, and a danish to go with it. And I bet I made him pay. I know George has no money, but he walked everywhere, he never took public transportation to City Hall or to anywhere. He walked. For dinner he had can of sardines. What did he spend money on, except a bottle of whiskey. He could afford to spring $1 for his secretary to have coffee and danish while he dictated his letters to her. LOL I bet George liked it. It made him feel like a real employer.

"You are a great employer" I said happily to George when he handed me my coffee and danish.

My dog loved George

I go to Republican BBQ Party on South Side of Town

(The whole Tucson Ron Paul Group was invited, so I was invited too)

I had an OK time at the Republican Party barbeque yesterday. It wasn't one bit what I expected it to be. I had delusions of grandeur when I heard it was a Republican Party barbeque at a ranch.

Instead Mitzi had 3 big picnic tables set up in her yard and we all trooped into her house to get the barbeque buffet. You walked thru the screened-in porch, past the alcove with the washer and dryer, thru the kitchen, made steep right, and she has the barbeque buffet set up there. Everything about it was homey to the max.

In the yard people were standing around talking, or sitting down talking. Apparently two of Mitzi's cats had kittens, because there were a lot of kittens walking around everyone. And the children were always stooping to pick up and hold one of the kittens. The kittens looked like they were having a good time at the buffet luncheon for the Republican Party.

And my vision of hot-shot big-shot rich Republicans was more or less shot to hell. Either they don't exist outside of my imagination or they were not at Mitzi's barbeque luncheon. All the people there looked like they could be on line with you at a Circle K, or standing behind you at check-out counter at Fry's supermarket. And by and large they were the least glossy people I ever saw.

The Ron Paul contingent was all at one table. I recognized them because they were all wearing "Ron Paul Revolution" T shirts. I don't say they stuck out like a sore thumb, but they were younger. And compared to the crowd at Mitzi's barbeque buffet they looked cool, hip, and sexy.

I wouldn't have longed to go over and be with them if the person I was sitting next to at table, was not the most impossible to-talk-to person I ever met.

Jim and I had arrived late. First because we started out late. He picked me up at 4:30, the buffet barbeque was scheduled to start at 4 pm. Second of all when I read the directions from google to Jim over the phone, he said "I know where Oaha is, all I need is the address." The address was 5131 South Oaha Avenue, so that is all I wrote down when I went to meet Jim.

He arrived at exactly the time he said he would, which surprised me, in the new car he had rented because his car was in the shop (again!). And it was fun getting in a fancy air conditioned car instead of Jim's regular car with no room to move and no AC. And Jim wore a brand new crisp starched short-sleeved shirt and chinos. I had never seen him dressed so nicely.

I had planned to wear a beige linen skirt and navy blue fancy lacey top. But when I opened up the closet door there was the plum purple velvet skirt with flounces at the bottom (ruffles) which I had never worn, and the black sequined tank top I had bought that time I planned to go dancing with Lily and Janey and had wound up not going after all. So I wore that with navy blue high heels.

I wore the necklace Lisa made and gave me, which is a large gold heart, which looks like she made it from gold tin a car ran over, with pretty red beads. It is a pretty necklace. And I stuck on turquoise earrings at the end. I couldn't find my lilac lipstick, so I put on bright red.

I put a pack of cigarettes in my purse, a lighter, a change purse with two dollars because Jim and I planned to stop and play the lottery on the way home, the jackpot is 300 million and Jim has his heart set on winning it, we plan to share. My bathing suit, I hoped there would be a pool there. And ten assorted size plastic bags, because Bill had asked me to bring barbeque home for him and the dogs.

Altho I had hoped Jim was going because he wanted to go too. In fact he was taking me because when his car plotzed the day before, Bill had driven him around all day. And in the morning, Bill had driven him to rent a car at the airport, and that was a long drive. Bill had taken one look at the directions on google and said "I will never find this place, ask Jim if he will take you." So Jim was taking me to return the favor.

Since Jim votes libertarian, and listens to right wing car radio when he is not listening to sports, I thought he would fit right in there. But on the way he told me, "I'll vote for Ron Paul if he wins the ticket, but he won't win the ticket, because the Republican Party will put their money behind the other candidates."

Then he said "you should have invited Alice, she is

interested in politics."

I said "Alice's guy is John Edwards."

He said "John Edwards is a good man, better than all the Republicans except for Ron Paul. Bush is a nazi and the Republican Party is all nazis."

I thought "O no! we are going to a party to elect Republicans, I hope Jim does not open up his mouth and say Republicans are all nazis."

Then he drove thru South Tucson. I recognized it. And when we came to a residential neighborhood behind it where I had never been, I guess this is the residential part of South Tucson.

"This is charming" I said to Jim.

"A lot of coke dealers are here" he said, and pointed out a house, and said "they deal coke there."

And then we arrived at Oahu Circle, which was a cul de sac and led nowhere. And we arrived at Oahu Road, which led nowhere. And we could not find Oahu Avenue which had our address. We rode around in circles three times. And finally I got out to ask a man working in his yard. I was surprised to notice there were no people out on the street at all, but this is understandable in great heat.

The young man was working in his yard, and boy was

he lovely! He was so lovely and kind and intelligent and helpful, that I thought "South Tucson sure seems like a nice place to live." South Tucson is where everyone lived until about 50 years ago. Where I live now was just pristine desert back then.

The man was lovely and helpful but did not know where Oahu Avenue was, and suggested we call cell phone information and ask them for the cross street. But Jim figured all the Oahus would be together, Oahu Circle, Oahu Road, Oahu Way, and he would find Oahu Avenue, which he eventually did.

I said "Jim, it is a ranch, how can it be on this road, this is completely residential." It was just houses next to each other, not big houses, not little houses, regular houses.

He said "In Tucson everyone calls their house a ranch, it doesn't mean anything. And you don't know what Arizonans are like, they are crazy, once in Phoenix I drove around for two hours trying to find a woman's house, I couldn't find it because she had named her driveway a street."

But finally Jim said "this is where 5131 would be," and there was a sign which said RD 51.

And I looked at my paper where I had written down the

address, it said "The Lathrops Ranch RD 51." And I read that off to Jim. And he said "if only you had told me RD 51 I would have found it a long time ago!"

Who knew!

So we started to drive on a dirt road thru desert, and then I saw a car with a Ron Paul sticker on it, so I knew we were at the right place, and then I saw other cars, and up ahead in the middle of the desert, we saw a house.

"This must be it" I said to Jim, "since we are only staying one hour, park where you can get out, and we don't get boxed in."

So he made a turn off to a tiny dirt road, and he was scared to death the cactus would scratch the car because then he would have to pay for it.

And I said "we'll walk even tho I am wearing high heels."

And he said "this is the last Republican Party event I am ever taking you to!"

I guess he didn't like getting lost on the way there, and he didn't like parking in the middle of the desert and being scared about scratching rented car and having to pay for it.

And when I leaned against the car to organize my stuff, the horn started to honk and Jim couldn't figure out how to shut it off.

So then we trooped to the house. A man was at a microphone giving a political spiel when we arrived in the front yard. But I just walked into the middle of things, noticed the remains of barbeque on paper plates on the picnic tables, saw people in Ron Paul Revolution T shirts, waved at them, and more or less said "I'm here."

The man was just announcing "last chance to put in your ticket for the door prize," so I went right over, and he unrolled one ticket and put it in the hat. And the woman said, "she has to write her name on it."

I said "I want another ticket for my friend Jim." So he popped that one in. I wrote my name on my ticket. And I found the one for Jim's ticket and wrote his name on it. And asked someone "where is the barbeque?" and they said "go into the house and turn right."

It was a lovely barbeque buffet set up in one big room. But of course my first focus was taking home barbeque for Bill and the dogs. So I made one heaping plate of that.

And then on another paper plate I put the small cream cheese sandwiches, the olives and cherry tomatoes, and slices of watermelon for me, and just a little of the chicken barbeque with barbeque sauce.

I piled both paper plates on top of each other, and tried to find a hidden place to transfer the big barbeque into one of the plastic bags to put into my purse.

There was a dark table in the dark kitchen we had trooped thru to get barbeque and it was deserted when I sat down. But instant I sat down people started to troop thru to get more barbeque, or to go to one of the other rooms in the house.

And at first I couldn't find a plastic bag big enough. There were two big tin foil toppings in sink, so I transferred it into that. And then discovered I had brought a JC Penny plastic shopping bag, so I shoved it all into that. And knotted it at top.

By then Jim had returned. He said "it is too hot to eat outside, I'm going to eat here." He had made himself a beautiful plate. And he said "this is excellent barbeque." He really loved it.

And a guy came in who Jim recognized. "This is Don from Access TV," Jim told me.

And I said to Don, "I'll show you where the barbeque is, do you want me to get a plate for you, or do you want to choose yourself." And I took Don in.

And I was going to say to Don "my friend Alice works

for Access TV, do you know her," but he was talking to Jim about illegal aliens. He was so heated on the topic. And I am so sick of that topic, because I used to be on a political forum where all they did was talk about that, and I think it is hate talk. So even tho, no way did I want to shove the big plastic bag filled with barbeque into my beautiful new red leather pocketbook, I had no choice. I did. And I went to finish my plate outside.

I saw the Ron Paul people over at one picnic table. But I thought if the Republican Party was gracious enough to invite us to their barbeque party, I should mingle with them and not go off and sit with Ron Paul people. Altho I had never met them and was curious to meet them.

Another problem I had, was because I was on political forums almost day and night for 8 years, even tho I am still immensely interested in the topic, I can't stand talking about the topic with people in real life. I want real life to be an escape from the topics on forums. I am happy to talk about any other topic but politics. There's been too much of it in my ears. I have heard every possible opinion there is for 7 years now.

I was sitting at my picnic table alone for about two minutes, when Don walked out. And I said "sit by me

Don."

I was prepared to be so friendly to him, because he was Jim's friend and Jim knew him. But no matter which conversation I started up, he did not respond. And even when I asked him a direct question, he didn't answer. When I mentioned this to Jim in the car on the way home, he said "you should have asked him about illegal aliens, then you couldn't have gotten him to stop talking, he is on Access TV every day talking about that." And I thought to myself, "it sure ruined his personality that that is the only thing he cares about."

It was totally hot in the house, they have no AC or cooler, and totally hot outside. And I was sitting with someone who refused to talk. I looked longingly at the Ron Paul party at the other table. They all looked so sexy compared to the crowd I was with.

In the buffet room the women were talking about their daughters' pregnancy, and what the sonogram showed. And I felt like I was at a Tupperware party.

I moved over to a table in the yard which had people sitting at it. And which, to my happy surprise, there was a fan going behind me. But the man next to me was deeply engaged in conversation with the man next to him. He was a little more glossy looking than the others and maybe he was an important person, because I heard him say "whatever I can do to help, I will."

Another man was talking to a woman who worked for the Tucson Library system. He was very upset because he has an 11 year old daughter and a 13 year old daughter who use the library, and he is very concerned people there are looking at porn on the computer and what if his daughters pass by and see it on the screen.

He said he has 6 computers at home and hasn't been to the library in years. "My daughters go because of the books, and I don't want to admit I haven't been to the library in years, but I am not interested in books."

The man at the other end of the table standing up, who refused to crack a smile when I gave him a bright smile, turned out to be the local head of the NRA in Tucson. And you could see the group around him felt very uncomfortable, because each one said to the other, "did you pay your membership fees for this year?"

The one wonderful news was instant I had filled out the two tickets for the door prize, one second later the drawing took place. And a man called out "Jim Reynolds! Jim Reynolds! Jim Reynolds!" Jim had won the door prize.

And when we were sitting at the table in the kitchen I said "what did you win?"

He said "I don't know."

They had handed him a small gift bag. And he unwrapped it, and it was a fancy calculator.

There was a beautiful big crystal ashtray right in front of me. And I thought "how nice they let you smoke." But I didn't want to dig thru all the barbeque in my purse to find my cigarettes. So when a man behind me lit up his cigarette, I was going to ask him for one of his. But I saw he only had 3 left in his pack, and cigarettes are so expensive now.

I said "maybe you don't have enough cigarettes to give me one."

He said "I am low."

I said "that is OK, I have a whole pack in my bag."

And I offered him one of mine, but he said he can't stand filtered cigarettes.

And I said "I understand, I don't like menthol cigarettes." And then we both said how badly cigarette smokers are treated.

"No other minority would put up with the treatment we get" he said. And I agreed.

But when he too went on a rant about illegal aliens, "10 dollars more a carton for medical care for illegal aliens! 10 dollars more for education for illegal aliens!" I thought "that's it! I am going to find Jim, time to go home!"

I went into the house and found a room where they were all sitting around watching a football game on a big screen tv, and I thought Bill would have liked it here after all, he likes to watch football.

And Jim was in the kitchen talking to a woman listening very sympathetically about how he takes care of his mother. Jim's mother is 98 years old and bed ridden. Jim does everything for her. He gets her up in the morning and bathes her. He makes her breakfast. He does her hair. Then he wakes her up for dinner. He shops every day and cooks delicious dinners for her. After she has her dinner he helps her into bed. It is a lot of work and in the morning his nephew comes over to help him get his mother out of bed.

The sympathetic woman turned out to be Mitzi, it was her house and her barbeque. And she instantly said "let me prepare a nice plate of barbeque to take home for your mom."

"And have you had enough to eat, let me prepare food

for you to take home too."

And she went in and prepared exquisite meals for Jim and his mom. She buttered buns for them, prepared a cup of barbeque sauce to pour over the barbeque, put in watermelon slices and cookies for dessert. The whole works! Prepared beautifully. Jim was overjoyed. "My mom will get 3 meals out of this" he told me.

I never saw Jim so happy in my whole life as we walked back to the car. "When I walked in" he said, "the first person I met was the Mayor."

"Did you see the Mayor?" he asked.

"No I didn't."

Jim said "I never met a Mayor before, I didn't recognize him, on tv he is short and fat, he doesn't look like that, and I told him if he needs any help running the city to call me."

Jim was overjoyed about everything. "That was excellent barbeque" he kept saying, "excellent barbeque." He had had 3 helpings. He loved meeting the Mayor, he was thrilled about it.

"Do you want me to take you back to meet the Mayor?" he said.

"No, that's OK" I said.

He was overjoyed about all the food he was taking home

for his mom. And he said he knew half the people there. Jim had a great great great time.

"So did you make any political connections there?" he asked me.

"No" I said, "I sat next to Don and he refused to talk."

"You should have asked him about illegal aliens, he won't shut up on that topic."

Jim found another route out, where there was a normal parking place, it must be the main route to the house. And a nice man in a yellow shirt, I had seen him wandering around the barbeque, I thought maybe he was Mitzi's husband, was getting in a car with a slender woman.

Jim waved enthusiastically at him and said "see you at the next barbeque."

And I smiled and called out "I had a wonderful time."

"That's the Mayor" Jim told me.

"He is?!" I said.

"Bill is going to be so upset he didn't go" Jim said, "he could have met the Mayor."

But I didn't think Bill would feel he missed out.

Jim said "I didn't vote for the Mayor."

I said "neither did I, I voted for Kimberly, she ran on the Libertarian ticket."

"Then I must have voted for her too, I always vote Libertarian." My friend Kimberly from swim pool had run for Mayor on the Libertarian ticket.

Before we had arrived at the barbeque, Jim had said "maybe I will meet a beautiful girl there."

And I said "I hope you do, Jim." And when he was in the house so long, while I was waiting for him to come out so we could leave, I thought maybe he met a beautiful girl in there. But it turned out he was talking to Mitzi who was so sympathetic about his mother.

I took a ton of barbeque home for Bill and the dogs but I forgot to take barbeque sauce.

"Here take this," Jim said, and handed me the paper cup with tin foil neatly wrapped around the top. Mitzi had prepared the cup of barbeque sauce for Jim along with the take-out she had prepared for him.

I was stunned with gratitude. It was the first barbeque I ever had. I understood for first time why barbeque is so delicious, why everyone raves about it. But what makes barbeque so delicious is the sauce on it. I knew the dogs wouldn't care, but for Bill it would be so much nicer if he had the whole thing. I was so happy that Jim just handed me the container of bbq sauce.

That's when my spirits picked up. That and listening to Jim's happiness. And of course it was fun to meet the Mayor in the parking lot. He looked good in yellow. He looked like a very nice man and sunny in yellow.

My spirits were going high again. But mainly because of Jim's happy joy. I realized never in my life have I ever seen Jim really happy. He's a wonderful guy, he deserves to be happy, and it is a great joy to see someone completely happy.

"You met the Mayor! you won the door prize! you got take-out for your mom! you had excellent barbeque! you are on a roll, Jim," I said.

"We'll buy our lottery tickets here on the south side of town, look at all the luck it has brought us, I am on a roll, now I will win the lottery," and he pulled into a Circle K.

His spirits were still sky high in the Circle K as we both filled out our lottery tickets. And the two women there were so nice to me when I screwed up my lottery ticket. I looked down at my black sequined top, and discovered all the sequins had come off all over my arms, and I said to the woman "and this is the first time I have worn it." I laughed.

I was just so glad to be in a Circle K and not back at the barbeque. I was glad Jim was in joy. And I was so happy with the free ice water loaded with ice they gave me. I was so thirsty and hot.

And we drove back under the most beautiful huge desert sky at sunset I ever saw. Only on the south side of town do they get a sky like this, vast and open. And Jim was swimming in joy and I was in joy for Jim till his cell phone rang. And I heard him say "She tried to commit suicide! Well what can I do? I am out west. Can't her mom help? Now they will take away her children for sure." He said "I am out west, I can't do anything." And when Jim got off he said his niece tried to commit suicide. He was very upset. He kept saying what an idiot his niece is.

After the phone call I guess Jim's happiness evaporated. And he became the same as he always is when I am with him. I never realized that Jim is not happy until I saw him so happy for that brief time. Because after the phone call he was how he always is, ranting and raving about everything under the sun. He said "all I want to do is get back home, smoke a joint, let the cat back in, give my cat her dinner, and go to sleep."

When he was still happy before the phone call, after we got out of the Circle K, he referred to me as "Miss Sparkly." I realized it was the only nice thing anyone had said to me for the whole barbeque. And I thought he meant my bright smile, but maybe he meant the sparkles which had come off my top and were all over my arms.

Jim had pointed out a Border Control vehicle on the way there, and said "do you want me to turn you in, you will get a free trip to Mexico." I thought I bet I can pass for a Mexican with my curly hair and olive skin.

Jim dropped me off and Bill and dogs all seemed very happy having their lovely quiet time at home. Bill was thrilled because the Cardinals game was on tv after all and had just come on. I instantly made 3 heaping bowls of barbeque, for Bill and the two dogs, and poured the barbeque sauce all over Bill's portion. Luckily there was a nice roll and soft butter on the counter, Bill could have his own buttered roll.

And I stripped off my clothes and put on a sarong and went to lie down in my quiet dark bedroom. I lit up with delight when Bill came in during a commercial to tell me it is excellent barbeque, he is so happy with it. And he informed me Beanie stole all of Lulu's food, and he had to give Lulu some of his. He made such cute jokes about Beanie, and Beanie stealing Lulu's food, that I realized when my husband is in an up mood, no one delights me more.

He was very happy to hear Jim had such a good time, and he even liked the door prize Jim won. "Good!" he said when I told him Jim won a fancy calculator.

In some ways it is easier to go with a man who is not your husband. When night started to fall and Jim realized he didn't know how to work the lights on the rented car, he was so blasé about it until he got it to work. I thought if I were with Bill he would have worried about more things. But when he made 5 jokes about Beanie in a row, it was so much fun and made me laugh so much.

I guess when push comes to shove what I got out of my outing, was the joy of seeing my friend Jim happy. And having a total departure from my regular life. The monotony of my days was really getting me down. But as I lied still in my sweet bedroom, with stuffed-with-barbeque-Beanie at the side of the bed, suddenly my regular life seemed like bliss, instead of something I wished I could have a change from.

Swim on cold rainy Easter Saturday

Easter Sunday morning 2009, 7:27 am

The sky is looking bluer and I think the sun is coming out. The ground is all soft and wet now from rain for a night and a day and a night, and I am sure the trees are a million times happier.

They did not have a drop of water to drink for a month and a half. For 6 weeks it was paradise out my window. Golden sun, blue sky. It was a treat unbelievable. And then out of nowhere in the middle of the night, the night before last, huge rumbling thunder, a huge incredible downpour.

And it never went away. The world turned cold and dark and very rainy. O there is a drop of water glistening on the leaf out my window. What a miracle!

Now there is a lot of blue in the sky and sunshine splashing into yard, but still dense white wet clouds over mountains. But I think the blue sky and sunshine have won the day, today may be a nice day.

It is so odd that for a full 6 weeks every single day was a glorious Easter Sunday, but now that Easter Sunday is here, it should be so trepidatious the way the sun and blue sky come back after their absence, like a timid knock at the door, so unsure of their welcome, when of course it is all we want. A tentativeness is the way it comes at first.

It was such a bewildering rainstorm, something out of nowhere like that, and interrupting paradise. You knew every instant it was a good thing. So much vegetation and all of it in green spring finery now. The plants have to have their water, their leaves have to be drenched. And the earth around them had turned very hard too. Now it is moist just the way they like it, moist mushy sandy mud. Roots like that, roots drink in their water that way.

Yes heaven watered the whole desert! And not sparingly either! Huge huge drenching rain, followed by another one; and then after that, constantly non-stop, for night for day for night, either sprinkling or raining or drenching rain.

Rain rain rain in total abundance. O that must be the quail pecking at the stale bread I put out. They are all out, the sparrow, the big quails with their red helmet and plume, I even saw my woodpecker. It is the after-the-rain breakfast buffet.

I don't think Bill and I would have gone swimming yesterday, it was no swimming weather! But the sign at pool said "all pools closed for Easter Sunday." We knew we wouldn't be able to swim today, so we grabbed our chance to swim yesterday. And I had errands I wanted to do on way to pool and way home from the pool if we were not going to go out at all the next day.

I had bought skirt at Factory 2 U when we were at Sunflower market on Wednesday (Factory 2 U is right next door). There had been 2 skirts, different colors and patterns but otherwise the same, and both were a size too small for me. But I was in experimental mood. I asked the girl at check-out "which one should I get?" and she pointed to the one with the blues in it. She said "it goes with more things."

I had been attracted to the one with the colors of autumn leaves, but I went with her choice. And there had been little purses made by "Hugs and Kisses," which had xxxoooo all over it. They were different shapes tho. And I let her choose which she thought was the prettiest shape and I got that. (O there is red cardinal! Sight for sore eyes! That flash of red! Absolute beauty!)

And to my surprise the skirt fit! Not really fit of course, I have to leave the whole top open, but fit enough so I can wear it. And to my huge surprise I love it, I love wearing it. It is a cheap skirt, no lining, simple inexpensive poplin, but maybe because of that I like its feel, so light and airy. And it just happens to have a nice cut, I look down and I like the way it flows. Instantly I wanted the other one too, I knew they were skirts I could live in all thru the hot blistering desert summer.

So when Bill told me yesterday morning he had tried to eat the spaghetti & meatballs I had gotten at Sunflower on Wednesday, but when he opened it up for supper the night before it was bad, so he ate the pot roast I had cooked for Beanie and had rice with it and made himself delicious stew instead.

So I said "good! we will stop on the way to the pool, I will get my money back for the spaghetti & meatballs and there is something I want in Factory 2 U, and then on the way back from the pool we can stop at the other shopping center, I will buy bread at the bakery, kitchen sponges at the hardware store, and books to read at the charity store."

The manager at Sunflower was wonderful to me. I had actually plucked the carton the spaghetti & meatballs had come in from out of the garbage can where Bill threw the whole thing, so I could show it to him when I asked for my money back. But when I got in the car I realized I had forgotten it by the sink. Bill said "Forget about it! Just tell him!"

The manager had a beautiful huge tattoo on his arm of the Goddess Vishnu, and on his wrist a beautiful big turquoise and silver bracelet. I told him the story of the spaghetti & meatballs, and showed him my grocery receipt, and instantly he said "Do your shopping and I will take the money off at the end!"

I said "I don't want to shop now, I want to go to Factory 2 U and then go swimming."

He said "OK, I'll write it all on your grocery slip and then you show it to them when you shop next and they will take the money off."

It was while he was writing on my grocery slip that I noticed the beautiful bracelet and tattoo. "What beautiful turquoise!" I said, "where did you get it?"

He said "it comes from India."

"O!" I said, "that is Indian turquoise, my own bracelets are Arizona turquoise and New Mexico turquoise."

I looked at it very carefully. "The bracelet is from India" he said, "I got it to go with my tattoo, it is the Goddess

Vishnu."

The tattoo went all the way up his arm. "Wow!" I said, "wow, that is beautiful."

"So you've been to India" I said.

"No" he said, "I asked my friend to get it for me, I wanted it to go with my tattoo."

O I get it now, he had tattoo of Indian Goddess so he must have asked his friend to bring him back beautiful Indian bracelet to go with it, and that is the bracelet his friend chose. It is beautiful, the silver work is lovely and there is a lot of it and it gleams, and many beautiful large turquoises.

Then I signaled to Bill who was waiting in the truck near Factory 2 U, I made my fingers go in a circle to show him it all worked out, success!

And I found the other skirt in Factory 2 U which is also size too small in the other pattern, and next to it another one. Neither is beautiful, neither is the one I am wearing now, but they are nice patterns and colors, and I just like the flow of them. And walking back to cash register I saw a pink purse also made by "Hugs and Kisses," and it was the day before Easter, who can resist a pink purse made by Hugs and Kisses.

The same girl at cash register was there. I told her I loved the purse she chose for me on Wednesday. She said "good."

"What do you think about this pink one?" I said, "I know it's silly to get two purses, you always wind up using one and the other sits there, but if you think it's very cute I will get it too."

She said "it is cute."

I said "OK, you only live once." And I showed her I was wearing the skirt she chose for me, "I love it" I said.

"Good" she said.

"So I am getting the other 2, it will be cool in summer."

"Yes" she said.

"I bought myself Easter presents" I said to Bill when I got back in the truck, "and the manager in Sunflower was very nice, he didn't want to see the carton, you were right about that and he wrote on my receipt to take the money off next time I shop."

"Good" Bill said, "Good." He was very pleased.

And we took off for swim pool. "O no!" he said, "I see lightning over the mountains, they'll shut the pool."

"We don't know" I said, "the pool may be open."

But when we got there there were no cars at all, I didn't

see lifeguard in the stand. And when Bill went to talk to them, they told him "we are on stand-by."

So I got out of the car to find out what that meant. She said "we will be closed for at least a half an hour and if we see more lightning we close for another half hour."

"Forget about it" I said, "I am not that compulsive about my swim."

And so Bill and I set off for shopping center with bakery, hardware store, and old books. "I'll buy the bread, I'll buy the sponges, and then meet you by the books." Bill had just finished reading *Tom Jones* which he had bought there and loved it so much. "It is the best book I ever read" he said. I knew he was looking for another book. And I had enjoyed the mystery by Patricia Moyes so much, I wanted to see if they had any more by her. We were both looking forward to looking at the books.

But it was clear as soon as we drove up, the charity bookstore was closed. It is St Vincent de Paul, I figured Easter was such a big deal to a Catholic organization they had to make a weekend of it. So I went to bakery.

The rain had started up again as we were arriving from pool to shopping center. The girl in bakery said her friend just called, she is staying with her friend, and her friend said "you left without your umbrella and your raincoat and now it is raining hard, I will come and pick you up." And she said how she appreciates it because as soon as she gets home she will have to walk her doggie in the pouring rain anyway. They must be living in an apartment if she has to walk the dog before and after work.

To my surprise Bill was in the hardware store when I arrived for sponges, he was getting stuff so he could start up our evaporative coolers for when the big heat arrives.

So then we reached home with our purchases and Beanie ran around in circles, he was delighted to see us.

Then to my huge surprise, Bill who had grumbled when we first got into the truck to go swimming, "I am only doing this for you, the last thing I want to do on a day like today is go swimming"— to my huge surprise Bill said, "It looks like it is starting to clear, call the swim pool! see if they are open! we'll go back and have our swim, if you don't want to go I'll go by myself."

"I want to go! I want to go! What a great idea!" I said.

I called the pool and they reluctantly admitted they were open and I could come over to swim. I understood their reluctance admitting it. It was freezing cold, terribly damp, very overcast, they did not want to sit high up on lifeguard stand and watch swimmers. They wanted to be warm cozy together in lifeguard house. I thanked him very much and said "I am sorry to inconvenience you this way" and he said "that is what we are here for."

We were sorry to disappoint Beanie but we were thrilled we were going to have our swim after all. And as Bill pointed out "now we don't have to make any stops on way home." And it really was freeing to throw down my purse, all my purchases, and just march out the front door free as a bird.

And my swimsuit was on under my clothes from when we had first started out the first time, so I said to Bill "here is my swim bag with shampoos, here is my towel, here is my clothes, leave it all by the bathhouse when you go in to change, I am just going to dive into the deep water."

The lifeguard still seemed a little grumpy when he came out to go up in lifeguard stand because I was going to dive into the water. He had been so merry and happy when he said "pool was closed" earlier on, he was not happy that now pool was open and he had to sit up in the cold and guard the swimmers. I said "I don't have to be guarded, I am a Junior Lifesaver, you can go back into the house, if I need help I will call you."

But rules are rules. When we swam at private club there was never any lifeguard, but at public pools, Jerry, who is in charge of all the lifeguards, makes them guard no matter what. Which to be honest makes no sense to me, as one of the lifeguards once pointed out "many of the lap swimmers were swimming before he was born and are better swimmers than he is." And in fact I found out many of them used to be lifeguards.

"Is the water warm?"

He was in no mood to gloss things over for me. "No!" he said, "it was a cold rain."

"Which is the warmest lane?" I asked.

"I don't know" he said.

Naturally I was the only one there. I thought "this is exactly what it was like swimming in the Adirondacks, I would stand on a cold beach before I went in, about to dive into cold water, with heavy dense dark clouds all around the mountains, just the way they are here now."

No matter how nostalgic I get for the Adirondacks, standing on that cold deck on dark cold cloudy day, facing cold water, I knew I would never return to that world. Once the girl has gotten a taste of sunny hot desert, she does not want to be cold and damp and chilly and uncomfortable; she likes to be happy in the warm dry sunshine.

But O I am so glad that Bill arranged for me to have my swim after all, when I had totally given up on it, I had decided it would not happen and I would accept it. It was such a surprise to be swimming when I hadn't expected it, and it did feel good to swim, to stretch out in the water, and the water wasn't that cold, it was fine. And I had long glorious swim.

And I saw another woman arrive for her swim. Pool is open till 4 pm on Saturdays, we had arrived at 3:20, the woman arrived for her swim 20 minutes before it closed. But she is smart, 20 minutes is not the longest swim in the world, but perfect for doing the trick. Bill was in lane next to me.

Few minutes before 4, I swam to the bathhouse, had nice long swim, and naturally at first it was freezing in there, there is no roof, and water in shower came out ice cold. But then it turned hot. Delicious! And I washed my hair and soaped up, and then went to the middle area, since there was no one there, to towel off, spray on perfume, and a little vanilla cream at back of my heels, elbow, and knees. And I dressed.

The girl lifeguard came in and she called out to the boy lifeguards "Don't lock up yet! Anne is still in here."

It turned out they had locked up everything. "We found you just in time, Anne" she said, "else you would have been locked in over night."

I giggled and said "then I would have been the only one who swam on Easter Sunday."

I felt glorious when I arrived back on deck, there is nothing like being all fresh and clean and all refreshed, and warmed up from swim and hot shower.

We drove home so happily.

"It's always smart to go swimming if you have the chance" Bill said when we got in the truck and were driving thru the parking lot of Fort Lowell Park. "Truer words were never said," I said...

Jim wins 3 dollars at lottery

Well this going back to writing is turning into an adventure. The first day, it did not work at all. The next day, it did. I was thrilled. The third day, yesterday, it didn't work as a story, but I made such an interesting insight in the middle of trying to write it, that I didn't care it didn't work as a story, my insight interested me.

And today I woke up right after dawn, before there was a yellow sun, or any color out there, and tried again. But it did not go anywhere.

But I'll give it another whirl today before I close up shop. It is still early morning, but more advanced. The sky is blue, the leaves are green, the sun is yellow, the birds are chirping. And I can see the black shape of my doggie taking the air, as she lies on the sweet earth, in first warm rays of sun. It is a very sweet sight, her black rounded shape.

I am here at desk, looking out back window into back yard, where Lulu is taking sunshine and lounging on sweet earth. Beanie of course is behind me, he likes to be wherever I am. And Bill is at other end of the house, trying to turn huge disused living room into art studio.

I got nice email from Eddie, Ruthie's big brother, who is darling boy. No matter what he writes me, no matter what the topic, no matter whether we agree or don't, I always wind up smiling at his email, and happy and thinking 'what a darling boy.'

It is a very unusual thing to be a darling. I love my husband, I dote on my own brother, I am crazy about Bill's friend Jim, my own dad was a honey-bunch. But darling is a very special thing. My dog Beanie is a darling and so is Eddie. Something natural and wild and sweet, all merged into one perfect package.

Like glimpsing a deer in the woods. You always feel like something rare and wonderful is happening.

Well Jim and I went to QuikMart yesterday to play the lottery. "It is 157 million" Jim said on the way. Apparently Jim handed in his number from last week for the woman to check, that was the day I could not play it with him, because I had zero cash in the house.

And then Jim did one of those dances you see them do on tv, a dance of triumph or ecstasy. He had won 3 dollars. And did that shuffle back and forth and swing your hips. It is the funny thing about the lottery. We always go to win 157 million and then jump for joy when we win 3 dollars.

"I won! I won! I won!" I exclaim when I win my 3 dollars and Jim actually did that little dance.

I have never seen Jim happy in my whole life. So watching that joyous dance had more beauty than a rainbow. There is something very special about watching a human be perfectly happy, you almost never see it. And it is like a planet jumping for joy. You don't realize what mighty colossal creatures we each are till you feel the impact of Jim dancing with joy in QuikMart.

Jim was a football player for the AZ Wildcats back in the day, and he did the dance football players do when they make a good play. It had sports written all over it.

Also Jim said on the way to play the lottery that he just got back from jury duty, and he got picked for jury, he didn't want to be on a jury but he got picked anyway. But "the prosecuting attorney is a honey."

I think Jim's spirits are finally rising. The prosecuting attorney is a honey, he won three dollars on the power ball.

I have never seen Jim happy, I never thought I would. No man has weathered as much misfortune as he has.

And two months ago, when his misfortune suddenly plummeted— it never occurs to you when you are at the bottom, that you could fall into a huge abyss and go so much lower— Jim did mention 3 times in 3 days, suicide. He had become desperate.

But just when things were at their blackest, there was turn. About two weeks ago, the turn began. He ran into luck instead of bad luck. Some things worked out, instead of working against him, he got a few breaks. And now he is dancing in QuikMart, and finds the prosecuting attorney a honey.

It's a start.

It's odd to realize Jim is now my best friend. I mean a best friend is an odd thing. He's Bill's friend. They have sports in common and go to the high school games together. And do big favors for each other, and watched Superbowl together. They have common interests and things to talk about with each other. It is a normal friendship. But somehow between one thing and another, I got close to him. Altho our conversation is only about what is on tv. He calls almost every day to say "just checking in, what are you guys up to, did you go swimming," and then we both say what we are watching on tv and get off.

It's kind of like having a neighbor back in NYC, just someone you feel close to and comfortable with, and are used to being around, and where you know a lot about their daily life.

Every once in a while they drop a detail which fleshes out their daily life for you even more. For instance I know Jim takes Maryanne's yoga class at the club at 8 am on Saturday mornings. I have known this for years, ever since I used to go to the club myself, which is where we first met Jim. But when I mentioned on the phone the other day "swimming is like yoga, it relaxes you," Jim said "but it's nice to socialize after yoga, we all go out for coffee and bagels together."

I had no idea Jim went out for coffee and bagels with Maryanne and the other members of his yoga class. It gives me a bigger picture of his Saturday mornings. That's what I mean when I say a best friend is an odd thing. It isn't someone you chose, somehow life threw you together. And your relationship is like a jig-saw puzzle, but one with big pieces, like a child's. Every so often a new piece emerges, where you know exactly where to place it, and more of the picture comes into show. And picture is always about how they spend their day.

"Were you able to go to the club today?" I asked Jim when he picked me up for lottery and told me he just got back from jury duty.

"No" he said, "but I hope to go tomorrow, I think the case will be over fast."

And then he said "court is so boring."

I know how boring court is which is why I was glad he said the prosecuting attorney is a honey. It was nice that something fun was taking place there.

Jim is actually the perfect juror to be on this case, whichever lawyer chose him knew what they are doing. The prosecution (I guess that means Jim's honey) claims the trucker had 17 drinks. But Jim said he knows what 17 drinks is like, and no way could the trucker have walked the straight line perfectly if he had.

"He had come out of the bar where he had been playing pool, of course he was drinking in there" Jim said.

"But so what! he walked the straight line perfectly.

"How do they know he had 17 drinks! They don't have any case against him, it will be over tomorrow."

LOL it is 8:43. That means Jim is there right now. With

the cute prosecutor and the hapless trucker.

Well Jim I hope all your wishes come true. You get the trucker off early. You get to go to the club today for your swim and steam bath and yoga, and to show your face. I hope the pretty prosecutor asks you for your email address, and I hope you remember how to get on email. You will discover email is a lot of fun once you start getting emails from honeys....Love and kisses, Annie

Girl in a dream

Friday November 6th 2009 7:06 am

This has been an intense autumn for me. First my mom went to Heaven, then almost immediately after, I found out she had divided the money unevenly. Lion's share to my brother. It was huge shock she did this, and shock my brother went along with it. I had thought we were close loving family, all for one, and one for all. As a result I have been looking at my relationship with my mother closely, going all the way back to day one.

I always had a difficult relationship with my mother (my relationship with my dad had been very close and loving, he gave me so much love, it never mattered she gave me so little). And it is true if my dad had not given me so much love, she would have given me more, because she would have wanted her daughter to have love.

Altho I spent my whole life working on my relationship with my mother I never really looked at it before. It was easier to see it thru a lens of fantasy "of course I love her, of course she loves me, I don't know why things don't work right."

Now I want to see it all clearly without fantasy. It is the perfect time because now she is perfectly happy in Heaven, back with her beloved Leon, playing tennis again, playing her flute in the band, going to the opera, long walks in nature, swimming in rivers, doing all the things she loves.

Since my mom now has all the joy and happiness I always wanted for her, it is the perfect time to be willing to look at and see everything I was never willing to see before.

I am not the only one having a major intense experience in my life right now, many are. I have been talking about it with Samantha, the head lifeguard at my pool. I don't know the story of her experience, she doesn't know the story of mine. We just call it "the intense experience" and try to understand its contours together. We talked about it again yesterday.

I wrote and posted this story on my blog today.

Life turns upside down
(it is like a big monsoon)

Well something has changed. There is some breakthru, something lightening. I can actually imagine my huge family drama drifting away like a big cloud.

It was so huge, till the moment I fell asleep last night, the hugeness of it still hit me, its unfathomable-ness, its hugeness. Maybe that was a big part of it, its dimension, its incredible hugeness. From first to last that was the biggest thing about it, its size, its hugeness. I was involved in a huge family drama.

But this morning waking up was not as bad as it had been the previous recent mornings. Whenever I had been waking up and trying to clear my head, had been so strangely difficult. I would wobble thru the house doing my waking up chores, putting up the coffee, feeding the cats, getting the tea water ready for tea. It was as if I was trying to screw my mind back in, like the way you try to get a lightbulb into its socket. My mind was in one hand, the socket was in the other, and bringing them together seemed like an impossibility.

The littlest thing seemed difficult and labor filled, just walking to the plant table with the big plate of tunafish for the cats wasn't easy for me. Finally after my chores I would stagger in to my machine, and after I started to write, things would click back into place.

I don't know how long this went on. I know yesterday morning I really noticed it. And then suddenly miraculously this morning, it wasn't. Out of the clear blue air, it just wasn't. Instead of big heavy dense wobbling, my mind was light as a feather, clear as a bell. I tripped merrily along as I did my chores. I didn't mind doing them, they did not seem herculean, they seemed a piece of cake.

I was not tremendously out of sorts, I was sorted out. Things had started to fall back into place for me. And when I sat down at my machine and looked out my window, the first thing I noticed was that the huge family drama, which had been wedged in the middle of my mind, had started to pick itself up and float on by, like a huge cloud.

It has been 8 solid weeks of incredible storminess, but now all seems peaceful. I look out on a peaceful landscape in my mind. Samantha at the pool described it yesterday, her experience of it, as "it's as if we had a huge storm at sea, it was an incredible storm, it was totally exciting, but now the big waves left over from it are just making us seasick, and we are looking forward to the relief of dry land."

For some reason Sam has been able to see the scope of this whole, right from the start. When I had my first moment of relief from such intense feelings, from all that intensity and storminess, I said to Sam "maybe it's over."

She said "It's not over, we have just reached the eye of the storm, the eye has calmness to it. We still have to navigate thru the whole other side of the storm, to be finished with it."

And she did turn out to be right about that. The eye lasted about two weeks. And it was some eye-of-the-storm! The feelings did not rage as much, it was not about rage really. It wasn't like being out in a tremendous storm, with the lightning thunder torrential rain and the waves, on the deck of the ship; and as Sam said tremendously exciting too, that this is happening in my life.

But I would describe the eye as far more intense in its own way, even tho it appeared so calm by contrast. The eye, where you see it all-- and what I saw was formidable!

Everything about this storm is so unbelievable to me. I

am amazed at what I saw when I looked at it all. Hahaha they say if you look at something closely, nothing is as bad as it seems. Like everything else about this storm, it was the reverse. Looking at it all was mind blowing. It was far worse than I ever could have imagined. It blew me away how bad it was, it couldn't have been badder.

But as Sam said "first to last this storm is all about excitement." This is not the worst experience in my life, it is the reverse, I would not have missed this experience for the world. This is an experience which comes once in a lifetime. Altho, as I said to Sam in the shower room yesterday, "once in a millennium." I told Sam I won't be ready for another experience of this magnitude till 3009, and Sam agreed, "same for her."

When I asked Sam yesterday "what it is like now?" she compared it to the monsoons we get here on the desert each summer. She said when the monsoons first arrive, those first monsoon storms, they are filled with such power. That lightning! That thunder! It is tremendously exciting and the power is not to be believed, it is huge. When monsoon season is ending, and the monsoons still arrive in late afternoon, they are not the same, most of the power is spent.

She said that is where we are now, it is the winding down of monsoon season. We still get worked up about what we are worked up about in this thing happening in our life, but we don't get worked up the way we did in the beginning. It no longer holds that tremendous power, and instead of being thrilled to be worked up to that extent, we are now looking forward to the relief of not getting worked up about it at all.

That is when she compared it to huge storm at sea and being on deck of ship and how exciting, but now it is like the big waves come and it just makes us seasick. As Sam said "we are so ready for dry land now, we are ready for it to be all over, we want to plant our feet on dry land which does not move, and walk away from it all."

Sam actually thinks this phase, the winding down of this monsoon season in our lives, will last this whole month, and then December and January are picking up the pieces and putting everything back into place.

I am more impulsive in my way of seeing it. I never see a whole picture, I just see it thru the lens of the moment. For me right now, I see a tropical island paradise with palm trees swaying gently in the breezes. I think I have arrived at dry land. But Sam has turned out to be right every step of the way. She always estimated correctly the huge size of this. If we go to Fort Lowell pool again today and if Sam is there, I will tell her I see the dry land off in the distance, we are that close to it, and see what Sam says.

But no matter what she says, it is heaven to be looking out at the island, to be seeing dry land, to be knowing this ocean journey is over. I wouldn't have missed it for the world, but as Sam and I both said to each other yesterday, we are both so ready for it to be over.

And yes I do think it was a blessing I had it. That is the interesting thing about this whole experience. What makes this whole experience absolutely different from any other experience in my lifetime, is it totally changes the meaning of good and bad experience. Before this I thought a good experience is when good things happen, a bad experience is when bad things happen. And I had experience to back it up: good things made me happy, a bad thing brought me tremendous suffering.

But this millennial experience now upended all of that. Because it would be classed as a bad thing, yet it was the most fascinating thrilling experience of my life. It was so dramatic, it was so interesting, I learned so much, it turned my life upside down, it changed everything. And the one thing it did not have any of, was suffering. Mazel tov!!!! To go thru such a big experience, to go thru such a "bad" experience, and have zero suffering, just thrills and chills, just the ride of a lifetime.

I guess that is why I feel blessed to have had this experience and that is why the monsoons on the desert are a blessing to the desert. The desert and every living being on it, every plant and animal and human, loves that season when the whole world turns into the most amazing lightning there ever was, the most amazing thunder there ever was. When the earth cracks opens and glorifies itself. The thunder and lightning show of all times. That is what it is, a great great great great show.

And then it is over and we have sweet paradise, and nothing could be sweeter, nothing could be more peaceful, nothing could be lovelier. Paradise is paradise and we love it. But it is the monsoons which bring this renewal.

And you know what, I think this millennial monsoon now in each of our lives, is completely renewing our lives. When it is all over, we will be brand new and ready to walk into paradise.

I love you
Anne

The End
Tucson Arizona, December 5, 2009

A note to all writers, cartoonists, artists, photographers, anyone who wants to publish a book

It is a great gift from heaven that CreateSpace and Lulu.com let any writer publish their book for free, if you do all the work yourself.

I was overwhelmed and terrified when I saw all the technical stuff involved, but the angels at the community board at CreateSpace walk all us newbies thru it. And nothing turned out to be as hard as it looked.

For those who have extra cash and don't want to do all this work themselves, there are many print-on-demand companies which will do it for you.

The beauty of it is now anyone can publish their book. A new universe has opened up for anyone who wants to share their creativity with the world.

Love, Anne and good luck on your enterprise!

Gal at pool and movie

More books by Anne Wilensky

Ruthie Has a New Love
published 2009

Soon to be published

More Girl Blog From Tucson

What Happened Next